The Mink Wrap In The Attic

Laverty Sparks

Edited by Tanis Nessler of ReVision Editing

Photograph by Larry Sellers

To my sister
Suzanne Jean Sparks

REMOTE POSSIBILITIES

"There's nothin' on this friggin' TV." The thirteen-year-old's words didn't need a tailwind. They came from deep in his diaphragm as he sprawled in the main recliner of the living room, surfing channels.

Elena Polson set up the dinner table in the next room, complete with bone china, silverware, and glasses. She was all for an old-fashioned environment in the twenty-first century.

According to Hunt Klyce, her life partner, he'd fallen in love with that trait, among others. Those included patience and understanding, an angelic voice, and the magnificent way she made love.

"Watch your language," Elena scolded. "It's not fit for moral consumption."

"At least I didn't say *fuck*," Decker Klyce half joked.

"At least." She expelled a long sigh as she checked the clock above the antique buffet. Hunt was late.

Again.

He'd probably stopped in at Paddy's Wagon, a local tavern in the college town they lived in. He was a regular, grabbing a few quick drinks before coming home.

She didn't mind—if only he would call to say he was going to be late. To share his intentions.

No, she didn't mind.

Do I?

After all, they had to wait on Britni, his granddaughter, anyway.

"Besides," the boy resumed the debate, *"friggin'* isn't the same as *fuck*." He let his body absorb into the chair as if he'd practiced tucking his bulky, sixty-eight-inch physique into small spaces. A lock of his hair stuck up in the middle of his head like an exclamation point. "Everybody says *fuck*."

The TV remote served as his new toy. It wasn't that long ago he'd given up his playthings, tears, and higher voice. "Everybody 'cept you."

She tilted her head. "Oh yeah?"

"Yeah."

She caught the characteristic sharp response. "Well, the point still holds that nobody in this house is going to get away with it. You know your granddad wouldn't like that kind of talk, and neither do I," she said, a combination of authority and irritation in her voice.

She stood back to survey the table, better securing the cotton strings of the red hand-me-down apron at her back.

Decker turned up the TV's volume. The room became no place for someone with a headache. "Right, like he's never said it. Besides, he's not here, is he? You're more liberal anyway."

"I'll take that as a compliment."

The teenager didn't give out many. Nor did his sister.

Elena would take what they gave.

Decker Klyce was a mass-produced Generation Z teenager in the stage of irresponsibility. He consumed a steady diet of television, smartphone, social media, and pizza. Not much else. Sports were out; he didn't have the energy, or the stamina. His generous, sloppy frame gave him an innocent disposition. Like the growing population of young people migrating toward obesity, he could qualify for a case study in that field. He was topping the charts for his height and weight.

"How could there not be anything on?" Elena quipped loudly to be heard over the TV and to change the subject. She placed the last of the knives at plate side. "We have one hundred and twenty-seven channels to choose from." She looked at him and squinted. "And could you please turn that down a few notches?"

She felt like a teacher, her soon-to-be step-grandson the pupil.

Childfree herself, she found the relationship with this dysfunctional family quite a challenge. She knew what she was getting into when she entered all their lives. Jony Klyce, Decker and Britni's single mother and

2

Hunt's daughter, suffered from narcotics and alcohol abuse and currently wasn't able to care for her children. She'd spent the past eighteen months in and out of treatment centers and jail. At the moment, she was in a nearby drug rehabilitation facility, drying out and making headway to recovery.

So when all was said and done, Elena Polson had traded loneliness for frustration and vulnerability.

Many days she wondered if it had been the right decision.

"Big deal. Nothin's on." Decker looked away from the fifty-five-inch screen to scowl at her.

The young man operated on a paper bag full of hesitation. He had dark eyes and hair and a heavy-featured round face that was moody as often as it was joyful. In her mind, Elena predicted he would eventually thin out and assume the suggestion of a Johnny Depp or Jon Bon Jovi, with a bit of Eddie Murphy's humor thrown in.

If this were the fifties or sixties, he would make a great beatnik. A great hippie, for that matter. That was, forty-some pounds ago.

But this wasn't the old days. This was the second decade of the 2000s.

And now, with an instant and unexpected family, she constantly evaluated the domestic situation with harmless curiosity.

Yes, Elena Polson had sacrificed her independence, her freedom, and her alone time to be with Hunt Klyce. He was that important to her.

But in the name of love, how much was she willing to mentally and emotionally give up? She had to figure that out for herself and put things into perspective.

In better times, she often wondered if they all would become *her* family someday. Despite all the struggles.

If nothing else, and as luck would have it, they gave her ample material for her freelance copywriting career. Without even realizing it. She was proud of the fact she made a decent living as an entrepreneur, renting a small office space in a co-working studio in downtown Worden, Ohio. She'd worked hard to establish herself in the community with a population of one hundred thousand.

Although the radio and television stations had their own copywriting crews, they still came to her periodically for her expertise. She also concentrated on print and outdoor advertising and brochures, and she had just accepted some internet website campaigns. A whole new scheme for her. Plus, every once in a while she'd do a voiceover for one of the radio stations she used to work for.

Life was good, professionally.

It was in her personal one she could use help.

She'd grown up learning skills of grace and etiquette. Lord knows what these kids were learning!

"I'm hungry," Decker said. "What's for supper?"

The promo to the Channel Eleven News was starting, and she took note of a thirty-second commercial she'd put together for a tanning salon. She remembered creating the promotion with spice and sparkle, with every intention of generating foot traffic to the shop. In her follow-up contact with the business, she discovered her efforts proved successful.

But why bother mentioning the accomplishment to this kid? He couldn't care less.

"Spaghetti. Dinner'll be ready in an hour." The mixed aroma of tomato paste, onions, and hamburger claimed the air, making her stomach growl. "Where did you say your sister went to?" She half looked into the next room at him, hands planted at her hips.

A heavy sigh beat his answer. "I told you. Cheerleading practice."

"Right." Elena concealed her anger, returning her attention to folding cloth napkins into oblong shapes. She had polished the silverware last week. She had learned the whole place-sitting ritual from her maternal grandmother.

And doubted the effort would be appreciated.

Every day she was peeling off more and more layers of hurt, anger, and disappointment in this setup.

She took a moment and reflected on what had happened to the guarantees of old. Those stockpiled feelings when she could allow her emotions to take hold and knew which ones to embrace. She missed them.

Thank heavens for the secret meditation sessions she'd come to cherish. Maybe she'd tune in for one before Hunt arrived.

The true colors of autumn were showing off outside the door and around the house. Mum yellow, pumpkin orange, scarlet red in the tints of a fading summer sunset. It was Elena's favorite season. Occasions to snuggle, walk in the crisp fall air, look forward to Christmas.

Yet the falling leaves also brought on tumbling spirits. She fought it every year, was prescribed the annual antidepressants. Age, too, was becoming a factor.

Her fifty-fourth milestone last month had passed without any hoopla.

This time she decided she would hold her ground, battle the war herself without any medication. Surrounded by loved ones, she'd focus more fully on her career.

So far, she had faced and gotten through the tears phase. Invested in herbal supplements to support her cause.

She had even gone in for an overdue makeover. Her shoulder-length, strawberry-blonde hair, sprinkled with a few gray strands, was now styled into layers of long relaxed spirals that engulfed her shoulders. She had also changed to shades of burgundy lip gloss for one of her staples. And she was pleased with the color trick the makeup artist had used to show off her almond-shaped eyes.

Now came the tough part. The impending winter. Five more months to go before spring.

Could she do it? Juggle it all in the name of sanity?

Would her sister, Pidge, be able to pull her through again this year?

Own your problems was her mantra. Words and lessons from her beloved mother, Doretta Polson.

"Gonna be on my PlayStation till supper." Decker's mutter thinned into the distance as he beat a retreat down the hallway. In the past few weeks, he'd pressed an attitude, becoming almost cynical.

Was it just a teenage thing?

Elena drew in a long breath and stood taller, relieved he had disappeared. She wasn't at all sure this particular relationship suited her as she'd never been through any similar experience before. Maintaining this lifestyle was already burdensome and perplexing. Central to the battle was Hunt taking custody of his two grandchildren—just three months prior—out of unconditional love and duty. Their biological father had visitation rights every other weekend.

Prized solitary weekends with her significant other.

So far, so good. It hadn't all been a total loss. But she knew trouble and guaranteed disputes lay ahead.

5

Both kids were at the age of tribulation. Especially since their mother was of no use and no help in her present state.

She had Decker halfway figured out. Or at least she thought so. He was just beginning his juvenile passage. At the fine line of arrogance, at the invitation into rebellion. He played Hunt, Elena, and his own mother and father for rights to a fledging adolescence.

Britni Klyce was another story. She was a tough sell. One-and-two-third years away from graduating high school, Elena's courtesy toward this girl's growing liberation hadn't begun to scratch the surface. Now and again it had a shape; other times, it went without showing.

Children. Something Elena Polson was in short supply of.

Even if she had any, what used to work didn't work any longer. The yesterdays she had been brought up in were long gone.

Life hadn't exactly turned out to be as simple as she had planned.

Being grounded today meant going without internet, personal phone, mall shopping, cable. These kids didn't know how to put up with inconveniences. In her day, punishment meant no television, telephone, friends, or playing outside.

Yes, she would have to orient herself on these youngsters soon, to the benefit of everyone involved.

Decker had left the television blaring. She went to the LED set and gazed at the program.

She felt as if she were a few decades behind, as if she'd been left out. And she had no desire to catch up.

Get involved with this crap on television now? No thanks.

Back in the sixties, her Dad owned the only appliance store in their hometown of Vaughn Springs, six miles away from Worden. With his knowledge of television repair, it had been a thriving business. She remembered when the music rippled out of the Philco radios he sold alongside the stereophonic units and phonograph records. But eventually the television stations added more and more channels and developed enhanced technology, putting him out of business.

Her memory of better moments cushioned the blow of this generation. Shows like *American Bandstand, Laugh-In, Mod Squad, The Carol Burnett Show, The Waltons*—programs that didn't draw a hard line toward morals and common sense, that didn't need to be rated—came as second nature.

She muted the volume with the remote and smiled at the mental souvenirs through the flat-panel screen.

Her reflection off the glass looked disoriented, with a slant of elusiveness. The vision was as if she'd driven through a torrential rainstorm and couldn't make out any bases. It was void of any reality, of any sense.

She turned the TV off as the six o'clock news commenced. No need for any more drama.

Elena was glad her prime had been in a different era.

"Hi, hon." The man she had given up her carefree lifestyle for came through the door. Hunt Klyce carried a six-foot-tall smug look in a study of brown: hair the color of country maple, clothes in light cocoa and copper threads. He had an endless supply of cool grins that had worked their way into her heart.

"Hey, babe." She turned to face him.

So much for meditation.

She kissed him fully and detected a hint of Jack Daniels. She was used to the smell that seemed to hover like an invisible cloud above his head.

And their relationship.

She was no stranger to alcohol. Her father had been on a first-name basis with all the liquor stores in town. She had to consider drinking to be just one of Hunt's few hobbies. And he could stand several more.

Get yourself together, she told herself. *Stay calm. No, it isn't fair, but you made this choice to move into his house, his world.*

"What's up?" he asked, gifting her with one of his winks.

"We're just waiting on Britni so we can have dinner." Someone else to wait on, she noted silently.

Those feelings were becoming all too familiar. Emotional tension built up, especially with Hunt's liquor consumption.

"Decker here?" His forehead puckered.

"Yes, in his room."

He strode to the closet and hung up his overcoat. "It's getting chilly out. I hate that winter's not far off, don't you?" His voice signaled strength and compliance.

"You know I do."

He should've remembered it wasn't her favorite season.

7

"Something smells wonderful!" He widened his eyes. As he did so, the small mole under his left cheek seemed to disappear. "I'm starved." He always spoke precisely and with a deep tone.

"We'll be eating as soon as your granddaughter gets here." Stress centered on the back of her neck.

Have I wasted enough time? she asked herself. *Can I get out of this role without consequences? Do an autopsy of my commitment?*

Did she have the strength, or guts, to leave this current life? To start a new one? Wipe the slate clean? Again?

Did she really want to?

This was all still new and could be rectified somehow. In the end, would it be worth her while to stick around?

Her woman's intuition played a return engagement.

Pausing in her actions, she calmly breathed in.

Held the air.

And exhaled.

NEWS REAL

In the privacy of his bedroom, which smelled similar to a well-stocked morgue, Decker Klyce sat on the edge of his bed and turned up the TV. He indulged in a triumphant grin and his heavy-duty pulse raced while he chugged a can of Coke without a shudder.

The report he'd been waiting for was making the top story on the six o'clock news. He had a stake in it.

Deep down, he loved the feeling. This was what made secret celebrity status. Plus, the local newspaper would feature it on the front page, no doubt.

Only he couldn't share his excitement with anyone. Ever.

He stiffened when the report detailed how another victim of a car accident, the third one in as many weeks, was the work of violators out to either get a thrill or actually kill someone. The local overpass was once again the scene of a dog thrown over the side and onto a coming vehicle.

"These malicious acts are criminal." It was as if the announcer spoke directly to him. *"Anyone with information as to who this felon is or these felons are, do not hesitate to contact the authorities."* The talking head bit off his words as if cracking nuts between his large strong teeth. *"Those responsible* will *face charges."*

Although the jab hit home, Decker nonetheless wished deep down they wouldn't refer to him as a felon. Unfortunately, that's what he was. He wasn't out to hurt or bump off anyone; the whole thing was just a joke—a joke more to his friend Scribes Cantrell than to himself.

He might be only thirteen, but he was old enough to know there could be serious consequences. But how could he get out of it now? Scribes would be none too happy if Decker backed out.

If the truth be known, he was scared shitless of Scribes.

The kid was just a mishap ready to explode, more than well equipped to handle trouble. He lacked sensibility and maturity, never sorry for anything he'd done. You couldn't pry him out of the long old army coat he wore even if a new one from a high-priced store was given to him. It was his trademark, along with the greasy black hair hugging his neck. His skin escaped exposure from any sunlight.

Decker called Scribes to see if he had watched the news. Together they had once more received top billing. What glory!

"It's great!" These were code words to let each other know they had both listened to the broadcast. The phrase was "just in case." Just in case anyone tapped their phone lines or eavesdropped.

But that would never happen. Neither boy would ever let it; they were bonded.

And if one betrayed the other, look out!

Decker honestly didn't mean any harm. He just wanted to be cool and brave like his school friend. To be involved with a cause and to fit in somewhere. He needed the attention that was lacking at his maternal grandfather's house.

His sister sure received enough of it.

He hated sports, would never excel in them or be an all-letter athlete. Sure, he suffered through television basketball and football games with his own dad. It was expected of him. Internally, though, he hated the competitive drive; it wasn't in his makeup.

Much to his father's and grandfather's disappointment.

He flexed his left bicep and with his right hand felt the softness underneath. He shook his head in shame.

Decker wasn't any good at bringing home above-average grades, either, and was far from being a national honor member. Once in a while, he'd get a good mark in science, his favorite subject. But the other studies he couldn't care less about.

So, when it came to tallying qualities, Decker Klyce was deficient in the impulsive column and was a volunteer isolate with no desire to mold into the social scene. An abundance of courage was nowhere to be found, even in the situation mentioned on television. He was happy just following his own pursuits. Like video games and the latest music.

Someday, he'd find his niche, get noticed in one way or another.

He figured he had plenty of time.

As for now, if it wasn't for his loyalty to, and fear of, Scribes, he would spread the word to his loved ones. He never intended to hurt them. Maybe he could let them know he'd made a mistake and find a way to right it somehow.

Yet he knew he would never be able to confess to the details. According to Scribes, the dogs he brought to the scene were on their deathbeds anyhow. Still, it might be interesting to discover just where he got them.

Certain aspects would always remain the friends' little secret. So he'd have to keep the triumph in his own mind. Be satisfied with that.

He paced the ten-by-ten-foot hardwood floor, making every step count. He turned off the TV set and smashed the empty pop can in his shaking hands. His stomach growled in hunger. He'd heard his grandfather come home and the muffled voices outside his door. He plopped on his permanently unmade bed and stared at the ceiling as he waited to be called for dinner.

Twisting his mouth in contemplation, he allowed his thoughts to focus on how his personality needed to change with each household. He was expected to act a certain way with his mother, a different way at his father's, and yet abide by the rules at his maternal grandfather's. Britni had adjusted better than he had. She had a few more years on him and was able to morph into the setup.

But at least his granddad allowed more liberties than his mother and father.

Of course, Elena was a different story; he didn't have much use for her. Sure, he strung her along to the best of his ability; stuck in this state of affairs, he had no choice but to treat his granddad's life partner with respect to her face.

Most of the time, it was difficult.

Common sense interrupted him as he reflected on the woman. It seemed as if she were constantly making a study of him. On the plus side, she *did* have values and morals, and she had accepted and tolerated the teens, no matter what they threw at her. Her modest manner was pleasant enough; she was all about getting everyone in the household on the same page. Ever the compromiser, she seemed adequately liberal, stayed up with the music trends, tried hard to understand hip language, and was an all-around good sport with all age groups. He'd give her that much. And she was always good for a tasty meal.

In fact, the woman was the total opposite of his own mom. His first impression of his future step-grandmother was that she was definitely more attractive than his mother, Jony. Her curvy, ten-pound overweight body was noticeable, even to a thirteen-year-old. And her heart-shaped face had gentleness to it, in actress Kirsten Dunst's sort of way.

Nevertheless, it was her sense of orderliness and kindness that drove him crazy. Like how she always wanted a full-course breakfast and dinner in order to make them special occasions. And she insisted everyone in the household be present so they could all talk about their days. Blah! He'd never been one to share, and she soon discovered that. Thank goodness that school lunches were reprieves.

Wriggling in the bed, he yawned and scratched his oily head.

And Elena always had the refrigerator and cabinets filled with healthy stuff, no junk whatsoever.

Come on, we're teenagers! We deserve junk! It's in our DNA!

Further, those times she gave him unwelcomed advice or set the rules for a proper way—her way—to behave sent his resentful attitude into a rebellious frenzy.

Nice try, lady! In case you haven't noticed, it's too late.

The mold had already been set. That pulse of obedience she strived for wasn't on his radar.

He found a hand mirror and noticed a new facial hair at his chin. *Glorious! . . . Not!* He picked at a chin zit. There were more on his face than yesterday. He made his expression change from curiosity to worry, and then back again to deadpan.

Pinching his nose, he threw the mirror down on the bed and returned to his thoughts as the essence of Italian cooking worked its way around his door.

Who did Elena think she was anyway? Those restrictions of hers didn't work in this household. And the sooner she learned that, the better for all.

No, he just couldn't warm up to her PG-13 state of mind and extreme sensitivity. There was a definite generation gap. Sure, he realized he should help out more with chores, but he knew in the end she would finish them for him. That was just her nature.

At least she didn't drag them all to church. That's where he'd draw the line.

He snickered at the times he'd tried to get her to cry. But she wouldn't. Or couldn't. Maybe she just smothered the tears, her decency acting like an adhesive.

What was with her?

Perhaps it was because of her copywriting business, always coming up with ideas for advertising. Heck, she even handwrote most of her notes instead of using an iPad or computer. He had no use for old ways, ugh! And several times she'd ask him how to navigate certain computer programs.

Who would've thought? An adult consulting a teenager?

And sometimes she expressed the need for ad material. Ironically, he was assisting her by giving her research without her knowing.

How clever of him.

Still . . . if she were more miserable, she would leave.

Right?

After all, she was the one who had imposed upon his family.

Hadn't she?

Yes, if Decker made it bad enough, she would take off.

His well of wishful thinking hadn't completely run dry yet.

As of now, his immediate plan was to avoid trouble with the Scribes situation.

Which was easier said than done.

PONYTAIL PROMISES

The next Saturday, Britni Klyce stormed from the bathroom, a scrunchy in hand. "This hair . . . this goddamn hair! Why me? Why couldn't I have inherited Mom's hair instead of Dad's?" The speech bulleted down the hallway as she plowed into her brother head-on. "Get the hell out of my space." She had a way with words.

"Good morning, sunshine," he said, stepping aside.

"Ahhhhh, screw you." Resentment sharped her tone.

"Hey, let's all just settle down," Elena called out from her bedroom ten feet away. Her statement sounded mechanical, rehearsed. She always seemed to be the referee, the counselor.

By default. By privilege of relationship. By benefit of age.

Was she indeed in control?

Or merely isolated? Trapped?

She thought she heard a muffled "Fuck you" from behind a door, but wasn't sure. Was she being censored in her own home?

Those standard apartments of old had been lonely, but she would welcome peace and quiet these days. Instead of constant chaos under one roof.

But that's where she found herself.

Both kids were a pain she could do without.

Could she honestly say it was a duty to manage these teens? They didn't act the same in front of their grandfather—they wouldn't dare.

14

Due to space considerations in Hunt's self-made, three-bedroom, eighteen-year-old ranch house, Elena considered herself fortunate they weren't underfoot permanently.

But they were there nonetheless. And the tension wasn't without energy.

She faced exasperation at every turn. In certain circumstances, patience wasn't one of her virtues.

"This house is too damn small for all of us," Britni said. "I'll be glad to get back home." She slammed her door for effect and a blast of hip-hop music followed seconds later.

So will I, Elena thought. *So will I. More than anyone.*

But that day was far in the future.

Jony Klyce had improved but was mentally and emotionally far from recapturing a normal existence or being able to care for her two teenagers. The treatment plan, this time around, was to wean her off opioids. She'd become addicted to the prescribed drug after a fall from an amusement ride while she was high.

So they all played the waiting game. Waiting for Jony to get better.

At the moment, the kids were in Elena's care. Hunt was watching a college basketball game at a buddy's. With her approval of course.

Again.

Oh yes, how accommodating she was.

He deserved downtime from his stressful position as a field construction supervisor. The cooperative November weather had stretched building projects beyond their standard limitations. So, he was continuing a rigorous schedule as if it were the middle of summer.

As she changed the bed linens, she triangle-folded the corners, knowing it would do no good on Hunt's side as he didn't like the top sheet tucked in at the bottom. But she did, so her side would be neat and tidy.

Come morning, the fresh scent of the laundry soap would have given over to Hunt's manly smells. She smiled at the thought. And three or four nights a month, the sheets ministered to their lovemaking.

Tonight wouldn't be one of those nights, not when the kids were in the house.

Would she someday learn to miss Hunt's fragrances? And the way he made her feel special?

"When's Granddad coming home?" Decker appeared in the doorway, startling her.

She checked her watch. "Soon, kiddo, soon."

Things had settled down. For now.

"Okay." He disappeared.

What was Elena to do? Hell, she didn't have any clue, no practice in raising offspring. She could imagine all sorts of possibilities quite nicely, but laying groundwork on this scale was a whole other set of rules. Her feelings toward the subject leaned toward inadequate, but were bona fide just the same.

She wasn't a veteran at being a matriarch yet. Entrenchment would take more than the two years she had been with Hunt. Yes, she'd known he had grandchildren, but semi-raising them had been a shock. She hadn't been ready or prepared to take on the responsibility.

Would she ever get used to it?

Why, oh why, had she agreed to help out those few months ago?

So far, and with luck, Decker had stayed in the background and not caused too much trouble except for his language.

But Britni was packed full of adolescent rebellion, enough for an executive committee locked in a stalemate.

Hey, maybe I can hire a mentor! She chuckled. *A guru for step-grandmotherhood. Someone who has the solution! What a revolutionary thought!*

Organizing socks in a dresser drawer, she took a moment and counted the years before her and Hunt's freedom. Sixty months to be exact. Until Decker was on his own.

The term could feel like a life sentence.

She didn't know exactly what kind of alternative was out there for her nowadays, but she knew if things didn't change, she'd have to find it. All she needed to do was convince herself what was best for everyone's sake, especially her own.

Until that day arrived, she would make do.

Goodness, how she missed her alone time. With no one to answer to and not a single soul looking over her shoulder. Being able to shop on her own, meet friends, read for hours before sleep, work any hours she liked.

As it was, she now had to follow a rigid schedule.

In her current mindset, she realized if she chose to stick this out, somehow she'd have to come up with a way to protect herself and inherently stay strong. All she wanted was to find fulfillment in a comfortable relationship. She'd found the man in Hunt Klyce. Now if she could just get rid of the other obstacles, life would be sweet.

Right?

She always managed to get by. Physically and spiritually, she had those facets under control. But, alas, the grandchildren had jurisdiction over her emotional and mental stability.

The point of living in-between may be closer than she imagined.

As she bent over the clothes basket in the closet, Elena felt the low-rise jeans she was wearing cut into her hips. With all the stress, in addition to menopause for eight years now, the pounds had slowly crept on even though in the interest of her health, she ate with nutrition in mind. She would have to add more walks and extra exercises into her routine.

Minutes later, she finished her chores, pulled back her shoulders, and padded down the hallway, hesitating at Britni's door. She knocked. There were more than a few seconds before she heard a nonchalant response.

"Come in."

When Elena eased the upper half of her body into the room, she found the seventeen-year-old sitting cross-legged atop her unmade bed across from her dresser mirror, trying to rein her hair into a ponytail. The sole window, with the sun on its back, provided the only light in the room. A song pelted from the small speakers of a boom box.

Elena's mediator role kicked in. "Can I help?"

Britni straightened the spine of her five-foot-four-inch frame and smiled, but it suddenly became a frown, as though she'd been expecting someone else. "I don't know what you could possibly do. This . . . this shit's a hopeless cause." She combed her recklessly dyed hair to the left, to the right, in a charismatic manner. She appeared to be in an impetuous mood.

Elena allowed the rest of her body into the room, pausing to survey the chaos. The place was at a loss for immediate revision. Strewn clothes and cosmetics, cluttered magazines, and two quiet strobe lights dominated the scene. It was the largest bedroom in the house, but it appeared contracted because of the lack of clear space. "Britni, it's a total disaster in here. I work hard to keep the house clean and in order. I would really appreciate your help."

She received a remote look from Britni. The girl had her father's nose and confident posture but lacked his finesse.

Despite the mess, Elena believed one day this girl would get her act together and make a great metamorphosis. In some circles, she would gain instant celebrity status. She would stand out in a crowd.

That's just how it would be with Britni Klyce.

Yes, she'd stumble a few times, but true to herself she would remain.

When the girl entered any site, a mental party began. Never one to be ignored, she was a one-person show, worthy of applause. She was spontaneous, flew in the face of convention, and was usually the first runner-up in a beauty contest. Her temporary hair color reminded Elena of the skin of an apricot. Normally it was raven. The profound chin suited Britni, while no fat rode shotgun on any part of her physique.

Elena doubted that naivety had ever prowled through her system. There was something about her that made her seem ahead of her time. As if she were born four years too late. In the long run, she would easily be able to care for herself.

Elena was sure of it all.

The girl wouldn't need the extra moments others required to adjust to the real world after graduation. She had the tendencies to figure it all out, and she wouldn't be pigeonholed into any particular group. She was in the top ten percent of maturity, and while her grades didn't qualify as prestigious, they ranked in the academic realm.

Elena cataloged her as one who would have affairs in years to come. In particular with men who would be nothing more than friends.

In the meantime, Britni needed to pace her dreams; she invested too heavily in wonderment. She was overly anxious, energetic, and restless about life. She may look the part, but her conscience went out of fashion.

The teenager was like a lark sporting her eagerness.

A song not yet composed.

She was unsure of herself as she pretended, and terribly determined no one should find out—especially those in her tight clique. Maybe it was Jony's plight that embarrassed both kids or gave them a case of insecurity.

Elena hoped that when the day came to prove the claims, the girl would have scruples to work with.

Ironically, Britni reminded Elena of herself.

No wonder she was worried.

"Care if I turn down the sound?" Elena all but screamed over the din.

A spritzer donated a sickening aroma of vanilla to the air.

"Guess not." Sarcasm at Elena's interruption sneaked into her voice.

Both kids were allowed liberty to decorate their sleeping quarters, and Elena didn't pry into their secrets because she didn't like it herself. Thoughts of her own room at her parents' hurried into her mind. Back in the day, she had kept tangible and intangible secrets hoarded away from others in her private domain.

Oh, how things had changed. Hadn't they?

What about the pictures of old boyfriends she had hidden deep in private nooks in her hope chest right now? Or the phone numbers of former love interests stashed in old coat pockets just in case she needed them if this present relationship didn't work out?

Now who was secretive?

Elena made her mind dash back to the task at hand, ignoring the answers to those questions. "Believe it or not, I used to have a ponytail myself." She piled a jumble of clothes from the floor onto the bed. Most still had the tags attached. Fashion was Britni's biggest concern at present. Maybe the clothes were simply part of her comfort zone.

"Oh, gawd." Using the reflection in the mirror of her dresser, Britni looked at Elena as if she'd vanished. "Really?" Her sulky attitude was in full swing.

"Sure. In fact, my best friend and I used to iron our hair." She cocked her head for emphasis. When Elena was Britni's age, life was like looking through a viewmaster, the slides in 3D and very photogenic. Memories worth keeping.

"Say what?" The reply was hard, almost in a huff.

Better get back in good graces now, girlfriend, Elena reminded herself. *Extinguish the agitation.*

"Yep, long before blow dryers, mousse, highlights, spikes." She liked educating the girl about days of old, whether it was appreciated or not.

Yet how do you teach this generation that life as it used to be was precious when they don't want to hear it?

Is it even worth it?

"I can't *even* imagine." She was about as interested in the conversation as she would be in a boring chemistry lecture. She listened to Elena with her ears, but not her mind.

"Just as a matter of curiosity, may I try?" She joined the girl at the mirror, sensing an undercurrent of hope. So far, a blind spot to tradition served as a patron.

"I suppose," she mumbled without conviction.

Elena combed through the reluctant teen's hair. It was as straight as the path to the girl's stubbornness. When the strands moved, they were like a jiggling hula skirt.

The color seemed to change according to her mood.

Elena wished she could've known Britni Klyce before she'd become so impulsive and callous. She guessed she'd have been in good graces with her in her younger days. All the girl needed was a few training tools for manners and her etiquette honed. It wouldn't hurt to boost her respect a bit also.

"To me, it doesn't seem that long ago. Yeah, we used a product called Straight Set." She stood behind Britni, hands at hips. "Nobody had curly hair during my high school years." Elena tilted her own head. "Sometime, take a look at my yearbook and you'll know what I'm talking about."

As if that were a possibility. More than likely, Britni Klyce would never search out the book or open it.

"So, what is it that you're trying to do?" She looked hard at her own reflection, noticing her eyes were a bit bloodshot and her cheeks were devoid of color.

"I just wanna look like Beyoncé, or Katy Perry."

"Oh." Elena recognized the names but wasn't sure of their hairstyles. If she were clever enough, though, she could make this effort pay off.

Do I want it to?

Can I really get used to this life?

Acceptance was very important, but only in the right situation. She'd been through enough rejection in her life that had left scars. Emotional wounds were one thing, deep blights another.

After all, it wasn't as if she could wish her life away.

When all was said and done, she wanted to be in this for the long haul.

If only it was just her and Hunt, how different things would be.

A small cloud of hope broke through.

"Ya know," Britni said, "chunky bangs, hair framed around my face." She paused for a thoughtful focus at her image. "The rest I have no problem with." She twisted her neck impromptu to inspect over her shoulder. When she did, Elena noticed a butterfly tattoo on her right shoulder blade, partially hidden under a white lace camisole.

Decker opened the door and peeked in his head. He released a giggle that menaced the space.

"Get out!" Britni yelled, electing herself as dictator with self-confidence.

"All right, settle down," Elena said.

The choice resides within you. Famous words from sister Pidge.

"Would you believe I also used to sleep with beer or soda cans on my head, just to keep my hair straight?" She gathered Britni's hair into a ponytail, then looped it around her fingers.

Quiet fell for a moment, vibes so obvious they could prickle the skin.

"You are kidding." Britni had a process of keeping her responses at a safe distance. "Right?"

Elena ignored the girl's smirk. "I am not." Her own giggle escaped.

Britni rolled her indigo eyes in disbelief.

"And, I suppose you were a fan of that one group, um, The Eagles? Or Aerosmith? Or God forbid, Hall and Oates?"

Their gazes locked within the glass.

"Oh, for a while. Did you know the best rock and roll band *ever* was Led Zeppelin?" Elena's look of reminiscence interrupted the action. But love for music didn't embrace the same appeal with Britni as fashion did.

The girl shrugged. "At least you are somewhat normal."

Funny, at this point in her life, she thought of herself as the opposite of normal in the presence of these teens.

"Jimmy Page . . . one of the greatest guitarists in the world." She fluffed Britni's locks, enjoying the background lesson.

"I thought Eric Clapton was?"

She hadn't lost Britni yet. At least the girl had an inkling of whom her future step-grandmother referred to. "Oh, there's several. Truth is, Jimi

Hendrix, Stevie Ray Vaughn, and Jeff Beck are some of the best. Ever heard of them?"

"Yeah, I think so. We studied rock music in school."

Did Elena just gain eligibility into this age bracket?

At minimum, she had created a new television ad in her mind along the lines of a musical generation gap.

Hallelujah!

"That's when music had all the makings of soul." Elena sighed loudly.

"Yeah, I guess it was decent enough."

Britni's anger had subsided.

Things will get better. We'll all figure a way out of our problems.

Won't we?

Would she make friends with Britni this time around? Could they ever share the same interests?

Should Elena listen with more earnest? Move from light conversations into the next level of more intimate ones?

Or would both of them lose the nerve to make something of their relationship?

All she knew was that she was tired of feeling as if she were trying to steady a stationary boat in a strong surf.

Inhale.

Hold.

Exhale.

Ah!

***

Meanwhile, behind the next door, Decker spoke to Scribes Cantrell over the phone at low volume.

"Can ya get out tonight?" Scribes asked.

"Yep, no problem."

"Good. I'm countin' on ya."

They would meet at midnight, when all in the house were asleep. The friend admitted he had already killed a dog out in the country for their next bait, the next conquest.

What once was a Halloween prank to the two boys had now become an obsession. Something more serious.

Throwing dead dogs, or ones near death, from the overpass out on County Road 975 onto cars on the interstate was cool. Just to see what would happen.

To them, it was powerful, almost ingenious.

They wanted to be known as The Silent Perpetrators. Local legends no one knew the identity of except the two of them.

They considered themselves to be like the heroes in some of the movies they still watched from their younger, not-so-distant days.

Pretending to be mercenaries to those mortal animals, Scribes and Decker would never be caught.

No . . . they were too smart for that.

They were too fast for the authorities because they had their routine down pat.

Their plan would never be uncovered.

No way would they be found out or suffer any setbacks.

The juveniles would never face charges of conspiracy to commit cruelty to animals or, to make matters even worse, attempted murder.

The two friends, Scribes Cantrell and Decker Klyce, were much too smart for that.

TREASURES IN HIDING

"Elena? Where are you?" Phyllis Morton yelled out from her kitchen.

"Up here, Pidge. In the attic."

Elena's sister lumbered up the stairs, past one of the guest bedrooms. A compact woman with an extra forty pounds, it was a chore. Her footsteps weren't exactly whispers.

On more than one occasion, Elena had tried to convince Pidge that a more plant-based diet would work wonders for her, like it had for herself, but her older sister wouldn't take the advice.

"What in the hell are you doing up here?" Pidge landed in the abandoned alcove situated above the house's dining room. She looked around at the modest heirlooms, the nostrils of her curiously flat nose spreading wide as she tried to catch her breath. A blue hula-hoop nestled in a far corner while a pair of white roller skates hung from a rusty nail near the lone window. There were plenty of other reminders of yesteryears. An antique dealer would be in his element.

"I'm hiding," Elena said. "You know this has always been my favorite spot to escape." Her mind locked up in the memories of this Vaughn Springs, Ohio, two-story homestead.

The attic had a life of its own, a niche where one would want to keep voices at a minimum. A solitary light bulb suspended from a worn cord served as a focal point. A beacon. A guide.

As if it were a medium casting a spell over the women.

"Aren't you cold?" Pidge adjusted her eyeglasses, which she claimed she'd never gotten used to. She had a way of staring into the distance, not looking at one directly, as if listening to celestial voices. This was one of those times. She had an expression of delegation mapped out on her kind round face. Physically, at two inches taller than five feet, she didn't have a commanding presence, but she made up for it in wisdom and thoroughly grounded hunches, and she was heavy on an unflappable temperament.

"No, not really." Heat from the adjacent room helped the cause.

"So what, or who, are you hiding from this time?" Pidge asked, putting the dry words into the bygone air. She shivered and sat on an old trunk, crossing her arms over her chest. She was almost colorless in the face, and Elena thought she could use a touch of rouge on her cheeks and red gloss on her lips.

"Life." Elena flushed. She was considering a neglected stack of 45 rpm records, quizzing herself on what was the on the B-side of the main label. Each one had at least one more play on them, despite the grooves in the surface from constant use.

"Oh dear, sounds intense." Pidge's small mouth puckered and she sneezed abruptly. Her dust allergies were kicking in.

Elena suddenly noticed Pidge full force. "Your hair! What color is that supposed to be?" She tried not to sound insulting.

"Chestnut." She fluffed her locks. "Why, don't you like it?"

"It's hard to tell in this light." She scrutinized Pidge's neck-length hair and a grin slid onto her face. "It's different."

The room's heavy shadows were being erased by the sunshine piercing its way through the only opening. The shut-off attic took on the look of a museum. Nothing had been disturbed in ages, not even the dust.

"Hey, look. Look at this." Elena put down the record stack and showed her sister her old silver flute in its original case. "Goodness, this brings back memories." She fingered the keys, which were in need of new pads. "Wonder if I could still play it?" She assembled the pieces and made an effort to revive the thirty-five-year-old accessory she had played in high school and during her freshman year at Ohio State. Puckering up, she placed her fingers in the correct positions and breathed across the opening. A shrill note let loose.

"Um, I think you need practice," Pidge said.

Elena snickered. "Exactly." She leaned the flute against the wall with care and looked around the space that was rich with reminiscences. She had long ago taught her olfactory sense to adapt to the musty smell of the closed-up quarters. "There are times when I want to stay here forever."

"That, my dear, wouldn't be healthy." Her older sibling rummaged around in the trunk she had been sitting on earlier. "Thank heavens we didn't have thrift stores back then, or Mom would've gotten rid of all this stuff," she said, sweeping her view over the loft, a place she never visited even though she lived in the house. "You know how organized and neat she was." Her breathing had normalized.

So had the temperature, thanks in part to the December sunlight streaming through the passage.

"Yes, she was." Elena's words were on the cutting edge of sacrifice. Benevolence descended upon her, the same way a sense of protectiveness surrounded her. In her parents' house, it was yesterday once more. Nothing or no one would ever take the feeling away. The legacy humbled her.

"Say, here's Mom's mink wrap. The one Dad bought her on their tenth anniversary." Pidge removed the shawl from its protective plastic and delicately inspected the brown rabbit fur. By all indications, she couldn't ignore the moment either.

"Oh, it's still in great shape." Elena also patted the soft fur. "Mother always looked like a princess when she wore this."

Both women relished the nostalgia by remaining silent.

Pidge donned the coat and paraded around. "Here's to the good old days of bobby socks, chenille bedspreads, record players, saying the Pledge of Allegiance at school . . ." She straightened and paused, seeming to labor in the name of tradition. ". . . Friday night at the skating rink and Saturday night at the drive-in, steaming up the windows." The coat was giving her a different perspective, acting almost as an aid to her speech.

"Speak for yourself." The gleam in Elena's eyes frolicked with merriment. "You had three good years on me."

Pidge let out a sigh and a small laugh. "How can you top those times?"

"They are not to be compared."

"Hmm. For sure."

Elena felt so comfortable with her sister that they could talk about anything. They were open with judgments, confessions, and gossip.

They never let each other down.

In Elena's scrapbook of life, Pidge was on every page. In their younger days, they were so close, they could almost share the same nightmare.

It wouldn't surprise anyone who knew the sisters that while Pidge was conventionally fact-oriented, cautious by nature, played by the rules, and anticipated the future and prepared for it, Elena's independent thinking, ambition, spontaneity, and emotionally oriented individuality lived to break those same rules, mostly in secret.

The sisters were proud of each other's accomplishments and were never in competition. Always in support. In good times, and bad.

"This Centennial age bracket has no clue." The tone of Elena's voice took a nosedive. "No respect or appreciation for the past. At least Hunt's grandkids don't."

Her sister found it convenient to assume her sibling's earlier mood. "Do I detect a slight bit of sarcasm?" She threw a sideways grin and delicately placed the wrap back into its protection.

"You have to admit, docile they're not." All of Elena's emotions were cued up. "I've tried to get through to them, make a difference in their lives, add to theirs"—she thumbed through an old Encyclopedia—"but I'm fighting a losing battle. It's like they're out of control, one step away from detention."

"You just have to give it time. Kids will be kids." Pidge's lips tightened. "We were teenagers once, remember?"

Elena nodded with benevolence. "Yes, but we weren't ever allowed to act that way. Actually, we probably didn't even think about going against the grain, until later on when we could rebel." She flipped through one of her old grade-school workbooks. "At least we had manners and were taught to say *please* and *thank you*, words sorely lacking in today's society."

"I totally agree." Pidge surveyed a handful of black-and-white pictures. "Hey, take a look at these pictures of us. In diapers—real diapers, not the disposable kind." Elena could tell she was getting a kick out of this journey, too, being around things of lasting value. "And ironed dresses. Remember Mom standing at the ironing board for hours?" She widened her eyes.

"Yep." Elena's mouth quickly twitched and tears formed at the corners of her eyes. "I miss Mom and Dad so much. Don't you?"

"You wouldn't believe. Especially living in this house." Pidge swept her hands up for effect. She and her husband, Bill, had approached Elena before the house went to an estate auction and they all agreed the Mortons would assume responsibility for the homestead that was located 6.4 miles from Worden.

"I'm so grateful you decided to live here and we didn't have to sell the house to strangers." She hugged herself. "Here I never feel abandoned."

"You're not abandoned," Pidge stressed, still leafing through the photographs. "Sometimes I do feel like I *am* the keeper of memories by staying here, though. It was a sound investment to maintain our legacy."

"Oh, Pidge, where have the last thirty, forty years gone? Or for that matter, where have *we* gone?"

There was a gap in the conversation.

"The same place as our figures, our money, and our good sense, dear." The humor picked the pocket of Elena's discontent. "We've traded youth for hot flashes, weight gain, and gray hair." She replaced the pictures and checked her wristwatch.

Elena's mouth folded into a smile. "But you still have your beautiful skin."

"Ah, thank you."

Talking to Pidge Morton was therapeutic; she was Elena's sounding board, making her problems easier. She almost always set her sister thinking in the right direction, had always been one to say the right thing. Each time, her timing had been impeccable.

The two women weren't exactly in sync, or always on the same wavelength, but most times, Pidge carried on their mother's wisdom and foresight. Yet no one would ever replace Doretta Polson. With her starched clothes, dazzling auburn hair, and a femininity that took over any encounter with her, the woman had been inspirational and kind.

In years to come, Elena hoped she would take on some resemblance.

"So . . . Apparently you are in one of your moods again. What's going on?" Pidge's lips dissolved into a straight line.

Tears again welled up in Elena's eyes.

"I don't know." She peered outside and focused on the dried-up flower garden and wooden trellis in the backyard. The yard had always promised peace. "Everything seems to be wrong. Midlife crisis, I guess. Time's slipping away."

Pidge joined her and hooked an arm around her. "Sweetheart, you're not *that* old. Not in this day and age. It's not like you're over the hill, ya know."

The speech penetrated. "If you say so."

Pidge stepped back and toyed with a silk dress of her mother's, the same color as the cough syrup the elder had given out for colds. It hung on a coat rack—intentional, dainty, protected by plastic. As if it was waiting to be worn again. "You have lots of good moments ahead."

Elena watched the neighbor's cocker spaniel dig in the frigid dirt. In the distance, she spied a tree house nestled on an upper branch of a twelve-foot oak tree. Sketchy clouds spread a thin web, worn through in several spots, across a faded-blue sky.

"Remember Mom in this? She was beautiful, so full of life," Pidge said.

Elena turned and brightened. She fingered the cool material of the sleeves. The taffeta was as smooth as the porcelain doll anchored in the corner. "I can almost still smell the Heaven Sent she used to wear. See the colors she chose. The way she coordinated her outfits." She straightened her spine. "Even in her last days at the nursing home, she never went without a coordinated outfit, complete with jewels and her iconic scarves."

Mrs. Doretta Lennox Polson had been a silhouette of modesty, femininity, and grace, possessing a cover-girl quality. Her hair had been elaborately and becomingly arranged, her skin had a natural softness to it, and she had an almost faultless figure, even at the end.

Fond memories of a lifetime ago.

How it had all changed.

For the most part, Elena tried to follow in her mother's footsteps. Ironically, the elder's once-secret wish to be a professional designer had guided Elena's life. Plus, she dressed in some of her mom's aprons and jewelry, and if she could have worn white gloves, she would. Unfortunately, there wasn't a single preservation of her father's she wanted to cherish.

He'd left his absentee impression on both girls.

"Pidge, where do we go from here? For me, I have the man I worked hard to get and, in a strange way, kids included." She settled into her grandmother's spindle rocker, which was stationed in the east corner. "I have a rewarding profession. My health is above average. I've been able to travel like I've wanted to. And, I'm having the best sex I've ever had." She didn't mean to blush, but she couldn't hide it.

Pidge snickered. "Then what's the problem? Maybe you've just hit a plateau. Met all your goals for now." She waited a beat. "Ever think of that? Besides, you'll have more. Trust me."

"I do trust you. It's just that I feel empty, detached. Of no use to anyone." She dipped her chin and looked into the wood-planked floor. She didn't care for the weakness she'd been experiencing recently. She was usually on top of things. It felt like unfinished business.

"Don't. Don't even say that." Pidge joined her sister at the chair, putting a hand around Elena's shoulders and forcing her to make eye contact. "You and I have a wonderful relationship. Hunt loves and needs you."

A cardinal steered onto the outside sill and began a tune.

"Besides, if something happened to you, I don't know what I'd do."

The two sisters had always been loyal to each other through thick and thin. Forever in each other's debt.

"Is there something you're not telling me?" Pidge backed away. "You're not sick are you?" Her face fell a few notches.

"No . . . oh, no." Elena's words were reassuring as she jumped up and returned the hug. "I'm sorry to have worried you. Goodness, I'm fine as all get out. As you know, all I take, as far as medication goes, is a multi-vitamin and some supplements." She failed to mention the blackout spells she'd been having as she didn't want to worry her. Or the meditation practice she still considered secret.

The cardinal pecked at the glass, and the women broke their embrace and looked over at it.

"But I *will* admit that no amount of healthful eating can take away misery. It's like . . . I've lost my spirit, my soul. Even my creativity these days leaves a lot to be desired." Once again, her emotions proved difficult to express in words. "I spend more time staring at the computer screen or writing tablet than putting down words." She walked over to the window and tapped on the glass, and the cardinal flew off. "I feel like the keys on my keyboard need to be re-padded, too, just like the flute." She pointed at the instrument.

"Oh, come on, now. I agree, you're just in a slump," Pidge said. "This is just a temporary feeling. A mere setback. You've had to adjust your priorities before, willingly, and believe me this, too, will pass"—she bore down heavily on the last two words as she closed the trunk lid—"once you've adjusted. Remember, we grew up on dreams of marrying the first man we bed and living happily ever after without having to work outside the home. At least we were pointed in the right direction." She drew in a deep breath. "Unfortunately, my dreams died, too, and the ones you had didn't live up to that expectation, either." She rubbed the back of her neck. "We make our choices and then live with them. Right?"

"I suppose. I think sometimes I feel this way because I didn't have any children. Whad'ya think?" Elena stood taller to lift an antique gold-plated picture frame off a hook. "Or maybe I'm just looking for a new normal."

"Could be. You've always been a wanderer looking for something more." Pidge pulled a smile out of the dimness. "Our little gypsy. You always had the need to run down the highway of life. Although sometimes it wasn't the wisest thing to do."

"Yeah, I should've chosen better roads to travel, taken better detours, that's for sure. But it's been a hellava great ride! No pun intended." The mood flatlined. "Yet I feel like my face"—she displayed the frame around her head—"is mounted in the wrong frame."

Pidge chuckled. "Hey, keep in mind, I didn't have kids either." She continued her crusade while she snapped off the light. "You deviated from the norm more than I did. It was like I was patterned—expected to be a nurturer, being the oldest. You were lucky, you had no set of rules to follow." She edged toward the door. "I just sort of kept a low profile." She curtsied.

"No, sis, you were the lucky one. You always seem to know what you want before it's even presented to you."

By trade, Pidge Morton was a successful financial planner in a local bank. Customers flocked to her, requesting her for her ability to work the numbers. She was the kind of person others came to for guidance.

She was married to an economics professor at local Central State University. True to her type, Bill Morton was intellectual. Elena liked him. He seemed grounded, perfect for her sister. Yet his personality could use an upgrade. He was too big of a man to be so small in optimism.

"If you say so," Pidge replied.

Both women had had plenty of false starts as soon as adulthood took hold. Elena's portfolio of impulsive relationships deserved to be documented, along with her two short failed marriages. For whatever reason, she'd never become pregnant, even without any kind of birth control. She'd never explored the available options, either, figuring it would be too stressful. Being childfree had worked in her favor and she felt no disappointment with the destiny given her.

"But why, oh why did I have to fall in love with someone with so much baggage?" Elena fretted. "His lopsided smirks and random winks get me every time. They're so hard to resist."

"That, dearest, is something you'll have to figure out yourself." Pidge stood at the door. "Come on. Let's get out of here before we turn into cobwebs too. Let's get some coffee. I'm so thirsty I could spit dust."

Elena laughed and made her way to the exit, but not before grabbing the flute case. "Should I go for broke and begin a new life?" She blurted out the question before she was ready for an answer.

Pidge shut the door behind them. "Good Lord, no, you've done that dozens of times. And here you are at the same crossroads. So, a new life is not the solution." They descended the stairs. "You just have to ask yourself what more you want. What more do you want out of life?"

The third step from the landing let out its familiar squeak.

"One more question and I'll shut up," Elena continued. "Do you think I have reached my potential and don't know it?"

They had landed in the living room, a much livelier part of the house. In the better illumination, Elena admitted she loved her sister's hair color.

"Until you know in your heart, only you can resolve that. And you have to believe in what you don't know." Pidge led the way to the kitchen and started the BrewMaster. "Have faith. You've always been full of indecisions. Passing through life in limbo." She opened the cabinet and stretched to retrieve two coffee mugs. "I've seen loneliness do strange things to people. It doesn't excuse everything."

Elena regarded the advice; it hit a nerve. "I know. So, whad'ya say you and I just stay up in that attic forever! We'll just make the rest of the world go away." She volunteered a grin, taking a seat at the dinette. "Live with the memories."

"Oh, sis, now you're being silly." She massaged her arms for warmth. "You're much too old to pretend any longer."

Elena really was on a roll. A whirlwind of feelings stormed through her. "Am I?"

"Of course. Sweetheart, life is as it should be. We can't change things now. Or make the world go away." Her voice tapered off. "Then was then"—she reached into her pocket and displayed a big shooter marble she'd brought from the attic—"and now is now." She rolled it across the countertop.

"And I need to own my problems, right?"

"Right. Just have faith."

Breathe in.

Hold.

Breathe out.

Life. Was it really as it should be?

Until she found out otherwise, she would have to accept that it was.

TWO SIDES TO EVERY PILLOW

Hunt's moaning was invigorating. Enticing. Infectious. Elena had always adored his sexual sounds. They were added attractions at every session, making her feel appreciated.

And . . . he always pleased her first, then himself.

"Oh, babe. Mmm ," she whispered, shivering from ecstasy.

The couple made love on a Thursday afternoon, three days after January had been inducted. The kids were at their dads for the Christmas break. Outside, a gentle snowfall carpeted the ground. Inside, the queen-size bed's sheets received a surface sweat.

A pine-scented candle provided the only light throughout the jade-accented bedroom. The couple had amicably chosen green, his favorite color, to decorate their sanctuary. On the spirit spectrum, she'd learned that particular color designates harmony, romance, acceptance.

How ironic to her situation.

"You are fantastic," he uttered. "You feel so great." A slight heat highlighted his cheeks.

He was deep inside her. They were one.

Briefly, she thought back to their beginning two years ago. Once Elena and Hunt had been intimate, they had both yielded to the curse existing between them. Back then, he was married to his wife, Gwen, whereas Elena was free of any relationship commitment.

34

Although seeing a married man hadn't fit her moral temperament, she had rather liked the temptation while still enjoying her freedom. It took them several false starts to slip into easy habits with each other.

But when his divorce was final, the guilt and reality set in for Hunt—blame and depression for Elena.

And she wasn't a fan of any of those synonyms for injustice.

At the moment, their heat and closeness sealed their undeclared vows.

His satisfied groans rejuvenated her recent poignancy. She had needed this connection with the man she truly cared for. Before they left for their dad's for the holidays, Britni and Decker had been almost unbearable. Challenging Elena at every turn, making her life miserable. She never liked being taken advantage of.

Were things so wrong they could never be right?

If only Hunt hadn't offered to bring the kids into the fold in the first place. Right before he did, she'd thought they were on their way to marriage. Now, she wasn't sure.

And after this new development, she wasn't certain it was what she wanted. She was a stranger to the fraternity of a ready-made family.

Genuine in his efforts, Hunt smiled down at her, licking his ample lips. A lock of his light brown hair fell over his left eye. "I'm so damn lucky." He lifted his chin. "You are all woman," he asserted between quick breaths, suggesting he was near completion. "Every other woman is just a female."

He'd used the line before.

It worked.

"Oh, Hunt!" She squeezed him tighter. Sometimes she just couldn't get close enough.

When he'd left his marriage to be with her, she'd had to make due, make things right with the decision. In the back of her mind, she always worried he'd return to his former wife.

Even though Gwen Klyce now lived across the country in Idaho, near her sister. She had found that there were too many problems to face back home and the more distance, the better.

And although daughter Jony needed her mother amid her transition, the feeling wasn't mutual.

Sad.

"This is perfect." She arched her pelvis with more diligence. "You . .
me . . . alone." The words came in spurts. "Perfect." Her speech trailed off
in an orgasm.

One thing hadn't changed over the course of Elena and Hunt's
relationship. They remained hungry for each other, losing their selves in
each other's juices, each other's sounds, each other's fragrances. Even at
their ages, intimacy was wonderful.

Unfortunately, both were still lost in his or her separate emotional battle.

"You're the best." Her voice changed from soothing to provocative, the
only time she allowed this luxury. "The . . . best . . . lover." She felt the
coolness of the 1,800-thread-count Egyptian sheets beneath her.

His kisses made a shortcut into her fortitude.

Nobody had ever made love to her like Hunt Klyce. No one had come
close. With all the trials and tribulations they'd been through, the passion
had never faded. It was their constant.

He was the feature presentation, the other men before him merely
previews.

The fact that he carried Native American blood in him complemented her
attraction to him. The dark eyes, romantic prowess, and solid build, among
other traits, gave her senses the inspiration they lacked in crucial moments.

Outside, the wind had picked up and a more aggressive snowfall pecked
at the window. It was nice to be safe and warm within his arms.

"Oh God!" He was ready for his finish. Within seconds, he reached his
climax. With the last shove inside her, she reached her own peak.

Each drew out a pleasurable sigh and a few seconds later, Hunt fell on his
own side of the bed. Soon, his heavy breathing relapsed into normal puffs
and his face restored its natural color.

In silence, she asked herself, like many times before: Why couldn't this
just be enough? Why couldn't she feel content? Settled down?

What was missing?

Wasn't it time she accepted what she'd chosen? After all, there were
worse situations.

Weren't there?

Can I find any legitimate loopholes?

Why are the kids the prominent downfall to this liaison?

Is it the selfish fact I can't have my own or is it their infringement on the lives of two more-than-mature people who deserve a peaceful existence and aren't getting it?

How long can I coast along in limbo?

Her mind fired off the questions like stones being thrown.

She'd need to figure in more patience if this was all to work.

Could she do it?

The furnace kicked on its cycled heat, adding to the warmth from the action.

"Wow!" Hunt searched for agreement in her face. "You made an old man feel young again."

She crossed her arms over her chest. The rest of her body was exposed. "Um, I believe I've heard that phrase before." She giggled.

"Okay, so I borrowed it." He slipped an arm around her waist. "Guilty as charged."

She rubbed his forearm. "But I must admit, that was fantastic! And besides, you're not that old at fifty-two."

He laid there in all his seasoned glory. For his age, he was still in great shape.

Did she really want to be free of this? Or was the sex just convenient at this point?

Right now, she could do without his infectious winks and musical muscles. And his grandchildren.

But intimacy wasn't everything.

It wasn't one of her priorities these days. She didn't know what was, but she knew even her creativity had suffered lately. All had become lukewarm in the heat of her middle-age crisis. She knew she'd have to adjust a few things to get back her mojo—or she could lose her copywriting business. Her spare time and energy should be focused not only on producing ads but also on editing, revising, researching, and marketing. Not babysitting teenagers.

Elena's eyes misted. She tried to excuse away the heartache one more time.

"Oh, hon, please don't cry." Hunt rose on one elbow, looking at her squarely. The man was a blend of understanding and compassion in those liquid blue eyes of his. She should consider herself blessed to have him.

"It's okay," she managed. "I'm all right, more than okay." She returned a smile and grazed the side of his face with the back of her hand. "They're tears of joy."

"They'd better be," he said. "Or else you'd have some explaining to do." He playfully nipped her earlobe, one of her erogenous zones.

"You make me feel so . . . " She paused with the fleeting thought of the impending kids' return in a few days. ". . . whole. Like I really do belong here." She hoped the words didn't come out as wailing.

"You do belong here, baby." He continued his part. "My little Miss Behavior." It had been his nickname for her since their inception. "Whew, you sure know how to please your man." He kissed her on the nose.

She noticed the pile of blankets at the bottom of the bed and shook her head. "You're silly." She chuckled and swept the loose strand of hair away from his forehead.

Their eyes locked for a split second, the romance deep within obvious.

Yet had that long-lost passion ceased to exist now for her? True, their sexual relations were beyond pleasing, but they had also become habitual. She had to wonder if that routine was the same for most folks their age.

"I love you." She went to work on the post-intercourse conversation.

"I love you, too, baby. You are my lady." He grinned, then suddenly grew serious, as if a shadow had passed over his mood. "You okay?"

"Fine." She forced a grin.

A full sigh stalled the response. "I'll have to take your word for it." He kissed her on the mouth. For some reason, that gesture seemed a little cruel this time.

She knew she needed to tell him how she felt, but she didn't want to break the spell. As of late, she kept missing the opportunity to open up her feelings to him, and she knew it wasn't fair to him to be this emotionally unstable about their partnership.

As she collected more thoughts, one stood out. His past filled her mind one more time.

Measuring herself mentally against the woman before her, she felt a hint of sadness at the fact that he once had been a man who had to leave Elena's side to return home. Back to his loyal wife, lying to her about where he had been.

Nowadays, he was a man honestly by *her* side. They were bonded. He wouldn't disappear from her side tonight. Or any night from now on.

Unless she wished it.

However, she couldn't get past that instinct of skepticism. Would he eventually do to her what he had done to Gwen? Lie about where he was? Break promises? Hurt her beyond repair?

Did the experts use the term *misplaced trust*? In the times she reflected on the matter, the suspicion caused her much sorrow.

Being with him, she'd given up the luxury of freedom and independence. Is that what she really wanted even after two years?

She could stay the course or bolt.

Did anyone have the answer?

Her mouth straightened in shame. "I'm tired, aren't you?" The question emerged from her chest.

"Yes, definitely." He shivered, gathered the chenille blanket around him, and returned to his supine position, soon asleep after all the physical effort.

From her own pillow, she studied Hunt as his snores punctuated the silence.

Even though she had spoken the words, when she thought hard about it, was she honestly in love with him? The deep, resounding, my-heart-will-break-if-you're-gone type? That obsession one felt as a teenager, that this would last forever and no one was going to change it? The she-couldn't-stand-every-instant-that-passed-without-him kind of sensation?

Deep down, she had a hunch they'd simply settled into a cordial surface tenderness.

Many times she asked herself if she even knew what absolute affection meant. For that matter, could anyone define the idea? Granted, at her and Hunt's start, the passion was intense, surreal, steadfast. In the beginning, she had used her heart like a canvas. Ready for decoration, ready for guarantees. Much like a campaign promise.

Had it only been infatuation, even at her age, when she had first memorized his eyes, his mouth, and how his hair parted down the middle naturally? The way he always smelled of Dial soap? How his touch made her light up inside?

When they had met at his company's holiday party—Elena's invitation coming after an ad she had produced for Shelby General Contractors—she had been no angel, far from pure. In fact, she had been dating two men at the time.

Dating only—no sex, no allegiances.

Since adulthood, she'd most always followed that pattern, trying to find some form of solution to romance longevity. She hadn't gone through the ordinary channels she had been taught: those passed-down patterns of finishing high school, going on to college, getting married, having children, becoming an empty nester, dying.

That regime never materialized or interested her because she had wanted something different from the traditional blueprint that lay before her. She never wanted her future mapped out. Thanks, but no thanks. Spontaneity was what motivated her.

Throughout the years, she'd never found a grounded base and had no responsibilities other than to herself. As the childbearing phase clicked by, she'd never pursued fertility treatments or bothered with birth control. By pure luck, she never conceived and wasn't tied down to regrets or mandatory contracts.

And she was okay with that.

No man had really gotten inside her heart, even after affixing two impulsive short marriages to her resumé. Her two ex-husbands had not been father material. And most of her former relationships had been very temporary. She'd made plenty of mistakes and learned from them.

Like Sam, for instance, who had a wood fetish; or Ed the babbler, who listened but never heard what she had to say; or even alcoholic Randy, who nearly killed both of them one night on a gravel road after hitting a ditch and crashing his car.

As she ruminated on the memories, she realized that the "toes curled" kind of love seemed to always prove a stranger. Add to that, by the time she'd found Hunt, her heart had hardened.

In spite of everything, he was the real deal. One who had been worth waiting on.

Still a bit overheated, she rolled over to face the wall and blew out the candle that sat on her nightstand. Was the flame's flicker ironically reminiscent of her and Hunt's relationship? First hot, then cool?

She peered through the thin smoke trail at the shadowy bookcase three feet away, full of self-help books and a few favorite literary novels. The words within those covers had been inspiring, something she had needed at the time she read them.

She covered up with the bedspread as her body's temperature normalized, along with her heartbeat. But her thoughts wouldn't let up and sleep evaded her. Immersed within her soul, she hoped that compromise of some sort didn't remain an uncertainty.

It troubled her to think this union might indeed be an insecure liability. It was hard to consider it an asset at this point.

Unlike the past, no one could possibly know what the future held.

She listened to Hunt's soothing snores and wondered what he was dreaming. When she'd first encountered this then-married man, the possibility of a relationship became not only unfamiliar but also puzzling. She'd never set out to snag him, he just persisted. Initially, she'd avoided his contacts, finding his intimidating manner to be somewhat of a turn-off. However, he could be very persuasive and she finally gave in to see what he was all about.

He had wanted nothing more than to take her away from all of the competition in her arena, show his superiority, have her to himself. But he was wedded and constantly struggled with his home-front obligations. It all had driven him a little crazy.

Eventually, he'd reined her in.

But the consequences were huge.

Even in times of tenderness, she vowed never to be a ball and chain hitched to him, never demand excessive conditions. Because she always held that ticket to freedom, her devotion would never be ironclad again. Thanks to the many men before Hunt Klyce.

So, she had to ask herself, did he deserve better? Or, for that matter, did *she* deserve better?

She nestled the blanket around her neck and twisted her lips. But the lump in her throat refused to disappear.

She knew his alcohol consumption was a major factor in their happiness. Elena never understood why he drank so much. And she didn't think he was about to divulge the cause. Did he even know himself?

Her eyelids became heavy, along with her body, as drowsiness finally set in. She was weary in more ways than one. Dozing off would serve her well; however, extra contemplation tangled her mind.

Was she settling for second best in this relationship? Just like she had adjusted her life decade after decade since maturity took hold?

She certainly needed a rebirth to bring back the way it used to be; a chance to start over, with no issues or worries.

In the end, was that what she was looking for?

Right now, with Hunt's grandchildren, Elena had too many problems to own. And the prospects weren't looking good in the coming days. Tolerance was one thing, imposition was quite another.

So those crucial questions she was asking herself would remain unanswered.

In the meantime, she would put her need for complacency on standby. Keep up the good fight, continue plugging away, stick around to see what happens.

She promised herself.

One way or the other, she'd get on with life and cope with reality. After all was said and done, she may have to chalk up this experience as just one of those things.

And breathe again.

Thankfully, she could count on her meditation, which usually grounded her. She didn't know where she'd be without it.

Another bout of tears issued.

She had to decide if they were happy or sad ones.

MALL RETREAT

One unusually warm Saturday afternoon in early February, Britni needed a ride to the mall. And, without voicing it, she needed a loan. Her school's annual winter dance soon approached and she was in pursuit of a new outfit.

Her sweet voice ignited a conversation in the kitchen. "Elena, are you busy?" She leaned against the doorjamb.

When she used that delivery, Elena knew she wanted something. There was always an ulterior motive involved, a competitive tolerance. She'd figured that out a long time ago.

"No, why?" she asked as she wiped down the granite countertops.

"Then let's go shopping." It was her favorite thing to do. Too bad she didn't have the funds to support it.

Elena peered out the window and noticed a gentle rain falling. "I don't know." She thumbed toward the gray clouds draping over the yard. "The weather isn't that great out there." And she needed to get in for a root touch-up at the beauty salon instead of going to the mall.

"Oh, come on! You need to get away from your chores."

The girl was right, she could use a break. And a truce with Britni. Perhaps it would be a positive move for both of them. She untied her apron's strings and placed the garment on the back of a chair. "Okay, let's do it."

Elena followed Britni down the hallway to their respective bedrooms.

"Can I drive?" Britni asked, pausing in her doorway. She had begged for a car, but as of yet, there were no takers. Her age on an insurance policy was the main factor, her brazenness the secondary one.

"I suppose," Elena answered with reluctance.

The two gathered their things and started out for the three-mile trip in the three-year-old SUV as rain continued sweeping the land. Most of the journey was on the interstate to the area's largest retail mall. As Britni whizzed past other cars, Elena had to remind the girl several times that she wasn't in any kind of race.

Yet she looked good behind the wheel. So confident and young, with eager, bright eyes.

Oh to be that poised, and unfazed, again! Elena thought.

They arrived safe and sound, finding a perfect spot in front of one of the anchor stores. Exiting the car, Elena realized her palms were wet and her knees shook. She wasn't used to riding along with teenage drivers, especially on rain-covered roads.

The mission began at one of the major retailers, in the junior department. Searching the racks, Elena spotted a high-collared, long-sleeved turquoise dress. She loved the color. She held it up for the girl's inspection. "Whad'ya think?"

Britni glanced at her as if she'd just stabbed her. The reply was swift. "You don't *think* I'd actually wear something like that, do you? It sucks."

Britni was in one of her moods, under protest. Much like a Monday point of view in a most dramatic fashion.

In an effort to stabilize the situation, Elena returned the dress to its proper home, aware she was only along for the ride, being used for strictly that purpose. Nothing more. Even though the girl had gotten her way, Elena was impressed with her energy. It appealed to her own once-spirited nature.

They continued on their quest and retreated into the main hallway of the complex. Elena grew conscious of the smells: the greasy aroma of soft pretzels and hot cheese, the sickening perfumes from the beauty emporium, mixed fragrances emitting from the candle shop.

Her stomach began to churn and she felt light-headed. The walls seemed to close in. She took in a focused breath, hoping Britni wouldn't be at this long.

As they passed other shoppers, most appeared carefree and happy. Elena wondered if they, too, were preoccupied with problems and perplexities behind their smiling faces.

"Come on!" Britni's beckoning voice interrupted her reflections. She was giving Elena a look of genuine scorn for lagging behind.

They landed in a bright boutique with the newest trends in fashion and jewelry.

Elena fingered a display of silver baubles. "Aren't these lovely?" She jangled the collection.

The teen was preoccupied with a too-short skirt of ruffles. "Say what?" she half-replied, her forehead wrinkled in question. Generational traces of Hunt's long torso lingered on her frame as she held the flamingo-colored dress against her body and glanced in a mirror. "Never mind, I don't like it that much."

Elena watched from the wings. It wasn't hard to tell Britni Klyce was better at commanding the stage than most of her peers, yet she lacked the clout of the upper echelon of her classmates. She was positive the teenager would learn some hard lessons in her lifetime.

But learn she would.

The fact that the girl was a natural in persistence ironically pleased Elena. She would just need to pace herself, take her time in growing up.

In a weak moment months ago, Britni had declared her wish to be a runway model. By all indications, she would endure blaring lights in her face and make the dream come true. She had the stature, the facial contour, the attitude. She would get a jump on the others and make it once she decamped for adulthood and found the influential network she considered necessary.

Elena's perspective had always held that if you had it, flaunt it. Britni had it, with compelling charm thrown in.

They set off for yet another shop. The trek was similar to trying to maneuver the aisle of a rocky airplane ride. *How much longer will she be? My schedule really doesn't allow for this today.*

And now nausea undermined the plan.

She felt similar to a promoter trying to fill a stadium for a losing team, or maybe distributing propaganda for a rebellious cause.

An announcement over the loud speakers alerted customers to a lost child, who could be claimed at the center's main office.

Elena giggled to herself that maybe they'd like another.

Britni stopped briefly, contemplating the remaining shops. Elena followed suit.

"You know," Elena said, "my mother used to make all my clothes." Her tone and the way she stressed certain words in a meaningful manner strived for serenity. "I remember her staying up into the wee hours—or back in those days, the wee hours of before midnight—even ironing, making the ironing board cover stale and hard with spray-on starch." She stopped short of saying "something you'll never know."

Britni shot her a tight, unenthusiastic expression while her sighs held weight. "She sounds like a wonderful woman. I wished I could've known her."

The element of surprise caught Elena off guard. *Did I hear her right? Are the invisible walls that had sprung into place between us crumbling down?*

She was pleased with the response, and the revived interest. The girl could be thoughtful—it had happened before—but Elena knew she wouldn't want to go on record as being soft or complacent.

After all, she must maintain that teenage attitude.

They window-browsed in front of another brand-name outlet. A strong fruity scent suddenly disturbed the air. Elena had to carry on before the smell strengthened.

Finding a nearby bench, she sat down. Britni did the same, not caring why they had stopped.

"Anyway," Elena renewed her spiel, "back in the day we didn't have places like these with hundreds of stores to choose from, only mail-order catalogs or the three department stores in downtown Vaughn Springs." Memories jockeyed into position.

"No way!"

Their eyes met fleetingly.

"Yes way." She felt better from the timeout. "And one had a round booth near the door with a clerk inside it. My sister and I always wondered if the lady ever escaped."

Her snicker wasn't reciprocated.

"We used to get a Coke at Woolworth's fountain or Hanlon's Drug Store," she continued, growing a smile. "It was such a treat in those days, not an everyday occurrence like now."

"That's nice." The girl was clearly ready to move on. "Can we go now?" The invisible wall was erected again.

Elena squinted her eyes for a moment and then stood. "All right, I'll follow you." Her stories weren't appreciated, so she refrained from adding any more information. She really wasn't being uncaring with the recollections, only trying to pass on the joy of that time period.

"You had it rough back then." Britni slowed down enough for Elena to catch up. "You must cherish those days because you talk about them an awful lot." She scored with the insult, checking her reflection in a passing window. "Like yesterday's headlines." She covered the betraying twitch of her lips with her left hand.

Once again, Elena drew in a deep inhale of patience. If she or Pidge had acted like this as teenagers, they would have been threatened with a behavioral facility—known as girls' school back then.

So why did she bother trying to get along with this girl? Perhaps someday she'd find the answer.

"I *do* feel so far behind sometimes." The words didn't sound right, like they were miscarried. "But if I had the chance to do it all again, I wouldn't change the way I was brought up." Pride stalked through her system. "Never. Only a few bits and pieces of my life." The temporary sickness had disappeared.

"How comforting." Britni's reaction now lacked passion and merit. At one point, she had acted as if she didn't mind Elena being along, but now she was clearly taking exception to the trip down memory lane.

"Yeah, I may be rusted a bit, but I'm far from worn out." She laid her hand on the girl's arm but it was quickly shaken off.

"Uh huh."

At another anchor retailer, they perused the aisles, landing at the jewelry section. Britni tried on a black-and-gold necklace. It didn't match her complexion. She'd be better off with silver.

"Oh, this is impossible!" She shook her head. "I can't find anything!"

"Maybe you're trying too hard."

There was no response and Britni exited the front door with Elena at her heels. She knew her presence hampered the girl.

They stopped at a small specialty boutique where every item was under size ten and most of the clothes didn't have even two yards of material total to their formation. Very provocative attire that was way overpriced. There were no dresses for a high school affair.

"Hey, how about this?" Britni held up a halter top that would barely cover her upper body. She could pull it off, figuratively speaking.

Elena took note of her enthusiasm. "Wrong!"

The rebellious look of vindication on the girl's face could have been patented.

"Just for the sake of argument, what exactly are you looking for?" Elena asked.

The remark hit Britni full force. "Say what?"

"A dress for the dance? Or did you just want to come to the mall?" She glanced at the girl, sure that mingled feelings of annoyance and admiration were showing through.

"Sorry I inconvenienced you."

Elena ignored the dig, realizing her patience needed a quick fix. "That's not what I meant at all. I just wondered if you had a certain item in mind. What kind of store should we be concentrating on?"

There remained nothing positive left in this journey. Frustration pulsed through her.

In between stops, Britni calmed down. "I've been meaning to ask you something. Do you think Decker is acting weird lately? I mean, more than usual?"

Finally, an amicable conversation! "What do you mean?"

"Well, I know my brother pretty well and something's up." Her voice bantered in amity. She waved at an acquaintance across the corridor.

"Yes, I have to agree." She tried for the sound of affiliation. "And it's more than being a teenager."

The girl smirked. "Yeah, you know how disruptive we can be." She stopped for a moment at a cosmetic counter, almost forgetting her mission as she stared touchingly into a counter mirror, entranced by her own animated beauty. Like she was an innocent bystander at a parade. "He's definitely up to no good," she confided. "I just know it."

48

Truce?

"I guess it'll all come out in time," Elena offered.

"This thing with Mom affected him more than me."

The confession stunned Elena. At Hunt's request, the subject was rarely discussed at home. But to hear Britni open up to her was a major step in the right direction, a gateway into a new dimension. Hope and dismay fought in different corners of her mind.

"I'm sorry you kids have to go through this. She'll be fine someday and you'll all be back to normal."

"Ha! We don't know what normal is."

She'd never heard Britni or Decker admit how they felt. As if the words would be weaknesses they'd never overcome.

Should Elena just accept her fate and this situation? Give the kids the sympathy they deserved from a dysfunctional mother's choices?

Several times she had pondered if they would someday call her Grandma. She knew they would never consider her their true grandmother. Gwen Klyce held that title, always would. That was all right. She deserved it.

What was the possibility they could be a family someday? Or would they just remain four people still living at the same address? Either option gave Elena the same feeling as swimming with a leg cramp.

Pained but determined.

They trudged on and entered another brand-name outlet, meandering throughout the passages. A flowing pistachio-colored satin dress deterred Britni.

"Wow! This is beyond cool. Don't you think?" A look of radiance came Elena's way.

She felt the rayon fabric and studied the tag. "Yeah, but look at the price. Your grandfather would no doubt object." Her resolve was wearing thin.

"This is just totally unfair!"

The bellowing words were about as subtle as a punch in the gut after Elena had taken the time to bring her all this way. *Unfair? What a joke!* She'd made every effort to be rational. If she'd been able to have a daughter, and she acted this way, things would be a lot different.

For instance, she would be taught respect.

Something this girl had little of.

"Would Granddad make an exception this time? Please? Knowing how important this dance is to me?" Her loudness made others around them take notice.

"Absolutely not," Elena whispered with force. "With our funds, there can be no exceptions." More of a reprimand stuck in her throat, not finding its way out.

Britni turned in a huff and stalked away from her.

"Get a job if you want the dress so bad," she uttered under her breath. Three weeks ago, without Hunt's knowledge, Elena had checked into The Temporary Assistance For Needy Families program, a federal plan giving states certain grants for grandparents caring for grandkids. Her thought was that monetarily it would lend a hand, help them be more self-sufficient. But the funds had run dry.

Guess they weren't the only family who had issues. Not surprising in this day and age.

Besides, Hunt would be furious to know she'd gone behind his back to even research it.

Elena was working hard to keep her anger at bay when an irresistible impulse possessed her. Her thoughts flew back to the attic and a possible solution to this whole dance dilemma.

She caught up to the girl, once again playing the negotiator. "Say, now that I think about it, I have the perfect dress for you." Her gaze darted around as if she were revealing privileged information.

Britni scowled as though she were under siege and continued to walk ahead. "I'm not sure I want to know what you have in mind."

"Just listen." She stopped her at a flowing stone fountain. "It's one of a kind. There won't be another like it at the dance." The dress she referred to was her mother Doretta's silk dress in the attic. Britni had about the same body size. And it looked better than anything she had seen so far today. "Now keep in mind, its vintage. Mid-calf"—she raised her leg and indicated the length—"reddish-brown trimmed with silver at the neckline."

She had the girl's attention.

"Lace on the sheer sleeves and hem. The back is lace, too, and loaded with silk buttons and a bow we could remove." She tilted her head. "Trust me just this once. You'll be the envy of all the other girls at the dance." She enjoyed a mental picture of it all. "You'd be beautiful in it."

Brinti's expression was noncommittal as she lowered voice. "I suppose it's worth a look."

Thank heavens Elena had seized on an issue that presented no difficulties because she'd half expected the girl to be appalled at the idea.

"Come on, then. Let's get out of here," Elena suggested. Anticipation claimed priority.

When Britni made noises in the direction of the exit, Elena nearly skipped beside her, even though by now her heavy feet felt as if they were grounded in quicksand.

The rain had let up and the temperature had dropped a few degrees. The potential for icy roads became a concern. Elena drove this time.

On the return trip, the stilted vibration kept pace.

"One question I *do* have to ask"—Elena glimpsed over at the teen—"do kids even dance anymore?"

"Oh, Elena!" The question was never answered, even cynically.

After that, the silence proved its might.

And so did the day. At least the queasiness had lifted an hour ago.

Twenty minutes later, they pulled up at the Morton house, and after realizing neither Pidge nor Bill were home, Elena and Britni entered and made their way to the attic.

"Why are we going up here?" the girl asked, looking a bit exasperated.

"Because that's where the dress is."

She did an eye-roll and shivered, which didn't go unnoticed.

Elena opened the attic door and a frosty blast greeted them. She retrieved the protected dress and brought it into the adjacent room, closing the door against the cold. Yet the musty smell lingered.

"This is what I was talking about." She unwrapped the plastic and held up the dress on its hanger. "Isn't it gorgeous?"

Britni stood back and inspected the antique. "Hmm . . . I suppose I could try it on. How old is that thing?" She pointed with a finger and jutted her jaw.

Elena took a moment to respond. "Does it really matter? Style is style, now, isn't it?" She stepped away so that the girl could change clothes. "Please be careful, it really is vintage."

"Okay."

When Elena returned, her eyes widened and she inhaled sharply. "Oh, my gosh!" The beat of her heart had quickened the second she saw Britni in her mother's gown. It was a reaction she hadn't planned.

Britni stood in front of an old stand-up mirror, sizing up her own loveliness. The close-fitting, delicate bodice and skirt in a shade of cinnamon followed her slim line while the battery of buttons lined down the back of the dress was lost in time. The outfit drew attention to her rosy skin tone.

Perfect didn't come close to the right description. It was more like *astonishing*.

Depending on the accessories she chose, the look could be original. Surely, Britni would have the sense not to use overpowering ones as the long-waisted taffeta dress was stunning by itself. She remembered she and Pidge pretending in it, always playing make-believe with their mother's frills.

"I love it!" Britni's words were genuine, like a special force had been sent in to unveil a hidden personality. She spent more than adequate time in front of the mirror, mindful of her effective silhouette.

With crossed arms and wet eyes, Elena disciplined an impulse to hug the girl. She wondered if she could talk her into wearing the mink wrap, too, if the evening in question called for a jacket.

In times like these, all Elena wanted was to fit into the realm of their family.

To not be the outsider.

"I'm so glad you approve of it." She smoothed down the hem and felt the cool material. "You look absolutely breathtaking!" She looked at the teen and noticed the contentment on her face.

"Thank you, Elena. You're right, nobody else will have anything similar."

Elena knew that fact was important to her as she didn't want anyone else to outshine her.

They looked deep into each other's eyes. The first time, ever.

Was Britni finally giving Elena a chance at comradeship?

She savored the moment, swelling in gratefulness. The turn of events proved similar to once again seeing an old friend you thought had died. Surprise and shock all at once.

The readjusted attitude was refreshing. It was a start.

The last time Elena had felt this good, this complete, was the time she'd finished a major advertising campaign and it had aired with success on television for two months.

Maybe not all was lost, at least with Britni.

Breathe in.

Hold.

Breathe out.

Love.

DEGREE OF DETACHMENT

Hunt feigned sleep, but with every passing moment, he became more alert. Jerking himself upright, he took in the familiar arrangement of the emerald-and-cocoa-decorated room. The oak dresser hemmed in the matching sleigh bed while two occasional chairs sat under the single window facing him.

The shabby-chic curtains and queen-size quilted coverlet were in Elena's taste; he wasn't a fan of flowers. But he had let her embellish with her own adornment, giving her carte blanche. Deep down, he really didn't care that much about ornamentation.

He was a guy, after all.

The nightstand clock read half-past eight on this April Saturday morning. The sun carved out its presence through a slit in the curtains and radiated on Elena's empty side of the bed. Much like a ray of hope.

Curiosity, along with disillusion, hurried into his system. He was aware of a cruel distance between him and Elena as of late. Once more, he went over all the same arguments internally, coming away with no solutions.

He hated the feeling.

He'd had a rough week at the construction site. Material hadn't been delivered on schedule and the plumbing crew hadn't sent in their specs. Spring had broken through early so the weather couldn't decide to rain or sunshine, derailing the deadline. As supervisor, he was responsible for every facet of the project, from manpower performance of each crew member to superiority of the work.

54

So it was hard to get a good night's rest any night of the week.

Aside from work, his mind had been running on the subject of Elena for several days. Upon consulting his long-term memory bank, her willingness and patience with the kids were taking their toll. He wasn't ready to tuck their affection and spontaneity into the same drawer as his worn-out shirts. However, his spirits were disparaged.

As he leapt to the floor, he knew the old questions still didn't have new answers. In the end, could they make this whole thing work? How much more was each willing to give and take?

Doubt knew its way around his brain. It was an old friend.

He snickered at the thought of how loyalty frequently could be a liability.

Retreating into the master bath and snapping on the light, he performed his duties, but his mind still churned. His conscience nudged him, hitting upon allegiance. He wasn't ready to dismiss this relationship yet.

He realized some women just weren't cut out to be satisfied. Or, strangely, they were born to suffer. Was Elena one of them?

In her deeper moods of suppressed despair, there was no reaching her. She was the kind who didn't volunteer many emotions or too much information. Maybe that's how she protected herself. It seemed as though every time she was cornered, she resorted to escaping, he reflected, shaking his head. She could use a dose of optimism at this point.

Couldn't he also?

True, they had settled into a domestic routine, but where was the intimacy headed? It seemed to him it had stymied; those familiar symptoms of passion had now become an unnamed romantic disease.

Turning on the boom box to his country music radio station, he searched through the pile of clean linens in the closet and chose a green towel and matching washcloth. She'd made sure he had his favorite color available wherever necessary.

Once, he believed he had the best of both worlds: a great career and a wonderful home life with Elena. He'd fought hard for both. Since the grandkids had come onto the scene, he wasn't sure about either.

Under the warm showerhead, his uneasiness intensified and jarred his thoughts. In recent days, he distrusted his emotions, a feeling he disliked. When he reflected on it, he always figured making good as a copywriter wasn't such a different proposition from making good in building a structure. Each profession was a matter of sportsmanship, of keeping on keeping on in the face of discouragement, of continually giving one's best and trying to make it better.

He lathered up and enjoyed the warm flow of water against his facial skin.

Granted, he and Elena didn't have the best of beginnings. And since then, circumstances had managed to put something between them. How many instances would it take to convince her she would be safe and secure with him whatever happened? He had done nothing but please her even though they each had a different order from the other. With their career histories—her expertise at writing and his proficiency at architecture—you'd think the dissimilarities would mesh.

He didn't understand why they couldn't. He was known as a great provider, so why wasn't that enough?

What more could he do?

He shampooed his hair, scrubbing harder than usual. Maybe he was trying to cleanse away all the questions popping up in his head.

Like . . . Should he make alternative living arrangements? Gently suggest to Elena she get another place? Push her to move in with Pidge and Bill till things could be settled? After all, his allegiance was to his primary family first. He was consigned to make good all the past mistakes. He had been there for the grandkids several times as their legal guardian, preventing Child Protective Services from stepping in. As long as he could take charge, he'd never let that happen. No grandchild of his would go through those channels.

Complicated as it was, he did it because he loved them and wanted them to have better options from what they'd been handed.

So despite Elena's compassionate and delicate nature, maybe he should just figure she wasn't any good for him.

He rinsed out the suds from his hair. A salty droplet of water caught at the fold of his nose. He realized it was a tear. "There's more to running a household than she knows," he said aloud. He sympathized with the fact that before him, it had just been herself with no responsibilities or ties. And he knew how important her freedom had been to her. She'd proven over and over again she could take care of herself and stand on her own.

Heck, he was a little jealous of that independence!

He shut off the spray and stepped out of the shower. As he dried off, he caught his well-toned image in the full-length mirror across the room. For an instant, the recollection of both his parents' silhouettes shifted uneasily in his mind. He'd never wanted to fall in that trap of their obesity and lazy lifestyle. Haunting him for years, he'd fought the possibility every day. His two brothers weren't that lucky.

Meeting Elena had been positive, since her healthy eating habits only enhanced his mission. To date, he had no chronic illnesses or serious conditions.

Except emotional oppositions. He really wanted to get past this stalled phase of their relationship. Had destiny simply put them here and then cruelly didn't follow through? Where were the experts when he needed them?

If he didn't love her so much, they would be done. He wouldn't diligently put his emotions to work to save what they once had. Integrating into his situation had taken guts and courage on her part. After all, a traditional family they weren't.

For that matter, who *was* these days?

He believed the pros would call their circumstances a blended one. He had to snicker at the term.

At the bathroom sink, with toothpaste in hand, he was ready to get more than a few bad tastes out of his mouth. Squinting into the mirror, a sullen look and conscience stared back at him. He noticed a few more gray hairs at his temples. Well-earned gray hairs. He rubbed his matching goatee that framed an easy smile.

It had dimmed recently.

In the old days, he'd worn his feelings like medals, displayed them well. But now they had tarnished.

Why must life forever be trumped up with new complications?

It was like constantly having road rage without being in traffic.

As he brushed his teeth, he continued his deliberation. Yes, his partner had every reason to be discontented. Hunt knew his grandchildren were a challenge. Hell, even for him! Teenagers being raised by fifty-somethings were not exactly a great mix, but he tried to set a good example. And Elena had inserted herself nicely into the situation, possessing a patience that proved admirable. She'd been a tremendous help to him; for that, he was grateful.

However, problems remained.

With Britni and Decker's mother in and out of institutions and their father with a new family of five, Hunt had stepped up to the plate and considered the task of assuming custody of his grandchildren to be his duty. The act was no doubt more out of guilt that his daughter wasn't capable of the obligation.

He'd never be given a Good Samaritan award, but some things you just had to do. And by leaving Gwen the way he had, maybe he was looking for redemption.

"Are you about done in there?" Britni's eager voice hailed from the other side of the door.

Startled, he spit out his mouthwash. "Just about," he responded. "But what's wrong with your bathroom?"

He heard her shuffling her feet.

"Decker's got himself locked up in there."

"Well, I'll still be a few minutes." His tone was harsher than necessary.

"Oh, just forget it." Her footsteps retreated in a stomp.

Patience wasn't one of her assets.

Her voice reminded him of Jony in her younger days. She remained his greatest accomplishment. In fact, he still carried around her high school graduation picture in his wallet.

When she was still under his and Gwen's roof at their East Worden home, his actual birthplace, he'd liked to look in on her while she studied in her room. Partly because he was under the impression it was a father's job to keep in close touch with his only child. And to a certain extent, the sight of the girl surrounded by books fulfilled some vague desire of his own.

Although she was a bookworm, she would, on occasion, oppose her parents and rebel against the Klyce's attempts at raising her with morals and values. Hunt blamed peer pressure and the rapid expansion of technology, while Gwen pointed the finger at her generation's overzealousness.

Years later when Jony's arms thinned and dark shadows formed under her eyes, he knew she'd crossed the border into the unknown world of illegal recreation and he'd lost her.

But when she got pregnant by Brent Dorsey, they moved in together and she cleaned up, they had the kids, and times were good again. Nevertheless, the demons were just too strong, and repeatedly, she slipped back into old habits and her fragility worsened. Soon after Decker was born, she found herself on her own again, struggling as a single mother in a complicated world.

Hunt was content she never considered giving up the kids. It would have been too easy. He and Gwen had helped as much as they could. And here he was on that familiar ground again.

Slipping into jeans and a T-shirt, his ponderings over Elena still twisted in his mind. He was grateful it was the weekend, that he didn't have to hurry to get to work. Then again, he liked to use the opportunity to catch up on the paperwork part of his duties. He felt guilty because it took away from quality time with loved ones.

He'd never wanted to follow his own father's pattern of being a workaholic. But there were only so many premium hours in a day.

Unfortunately.

Adding his wallet and keys to his pockets, he glanced over at the disheveled bed and hurried over to make it. He borrowed a grin from his reserves.

When Elena had crossed his path, he'd been so in lust over her that reality took a sabbatical and he could barely function. She'd been a poison there was no antidote for. He swore humility and joked that his toes even curled. He was never indifferent to her sexual aura, simple pleasures, and gentle patience; those traits never stopped arresting his senses as they had gone straight and deep into his heart.

At the holiday party where he'd first met her, it had seemed as if the enticing music and dim lights had mesmerized him, setting the scene for their merger. No one else's presence in the room had even mattered. Their eye contact through the intimate glow of candles was obvious. They had toasted each other across the room with uncanny voltage.

He knew right then his life had changed.

But an important factor stood firm.

His marriage.

That was nearly four years ago. Yet the memory was still fresh.

Hunt lay back down on the mattress, held prisoner by the reminiscences. He shut his eyes for a moment.

He recalled when he couldn't wait to brag to his friends and co-workers how he'd met *the* woman, the one who would make all the difference. He could see what others saw. Her whole look wasn't magnetic on an elegance scale, only low-key on the whimsical gauge.

Which was fine by him, as he wanted her all to himself.

On the surface, what attracted him were her wavy, strawberry-blonde tresses that boasted more red highlights than blonde. He'd never seen hair that color. Her soft creamy skin sheltered a sixty-four-inch frame that wasn't skinny but not too fat either. He could tell she led a healthy regimen and would benefit from a tan.

And the hazel eyes, almost the color of copper, were her most noticeable characteristic. They were the kind that drew others in to her quiet charisma, unbeknownst to her.

He was shocked when she had told him her age as she looked younger by at least ten years.

The only visible flaws were her pale skin, a small mole on the top of her forehead, and ears that protruded a little too much. The latter two she kept hidden under her hair, with bangs and a shoulder-length style.

At the heart of it all, however, was her old-school uniqueness and how she always aimed to please. He loved it; it made her who she was. Her fashion sense was decades behind what was current, but she pulled it off with second-hand clothes and class. Hell, she even opted for aprons and handkerchiefs and washed dishes by hand. Thank goodness she couldn't stand to sew, or she'd probably make her own clothes. Her practice of still working on a ten-year-old desktop computer wasn't surprising to him. So far, she hadn't bought in to a smartphone, iPad, iPod, or online banking, typecasting her into an enduring category all by itself.

In this day and age, she was heavy on her timeworn ways and insisted on quality, never quantity.

He opened his eyes with merriment.

He knew if they still sold those old green stamps, she'd save them to buy products. He admired her economical sense of thrift and budget, certain the practice was passed down from her mother, who'd had the ability and skill to save and pinch pennies. Or so Elena said.

In some circles, he supposed she would be considered a minimalist. Off the grid.

He smiled in admiration of these pure virtues central to her appeal and his instant attraction.

But the downside of her withdrawal and hesitation was that they proved to be deterrents. They didn't exactly flirt with any success. He'd almost forgotten the pleasant sound of her spontaneous laughter.

Getting up, he padded to the bureau and slipped on his watch. For an instant, he caught a whiff of her body scent. Taking in a deep breath, he furrowed his brow.

He assured himself that there must be something else to reinforce his and Elena's love. He denied her very little. Would setting her up in another place soften the fall of all the obligations she'd taken on? An equitable arrangement might fit the bill; she just may agree to it.

He paused at the closed doorway. Before opening it, he deflected his thoughts to the night of Britni's formal dance. To how Elena had chosen the perfect dress for her—her own mother's. The stunning effect had captivated all who observed. The image worked around his brain. His granddaughter had looked every inch a debutante with Elena's guidance.

It pleased him how the two girls had made it happen. Was progress being made? Or was the act simply another temporary tactic just to get by?

Turning the knob, he stepped into the hall. Who knew what was waiting for him?

For now, more consideration would have to wait.

An imminent decision confirmed an ambitious enemy.

Maybe he should pressure her into an understanding. Because he had to know if Elena Polson's devotion was reliable and permanent. He was tired of the tide of doubts threatening to drown him.

He'd make an effort to pin her down for a further commitment.

For everyone's sake.

Especially his own.

NO STONE UNTURNED

Pidge Morton drove along the mature tree-lined street in Vaughn Springs and pulled up to her house. She noticed Elena's car sitting out front. Why was she here at this hour?

Slipping from her four-door sedan, she heard a melody from a flute playing in the distance. Was that her sister practicing?

Inside, she almost tripped over a kitchen chair on her way to the light switch. The day had turned old without any lighting in this part of the house. Years ago, the sisters had proposed the tradition of setting a chair in front of the stove to signal Elena's presence.

"Elena?"

Why was she here at this hour?

Pidge hoped she wouldn't have to deal with any stress or drama. She'd had a rough time at work today. Yet she didn't want to disappoint her baby sister, either, who was her only close relative. She knew she was Elena's constant, her "go-to person."

And she never wanted to let her down. She remembered that after leaving home to attend college, Elena had exhibited the first signs of depression. She had drifted into an emotional emptiness of fatigue and restlessness. Her parents didn't know how to cope with the despair because the resources back then weren't what they were today.

Before she went upstairs, Pidge started the teapot on the stove. It was their ritual.

She couldn't help wondering why Elena had been spending an awful lot of time at her house. There must be something amiss for her sister to retreat into the attic so often.

After all, she should be an expert at the signs. She'd been through it before. With utmost predictability, every autumn brought on Elena's seasonal affective disorder. Heck, she had a touch of it herself each year.

But this was May. What was going on?

She had a feeling Elena was on the verge of losing her business. That would be catastrophic to her psyche. Not to mention her pocketbook.

"Hi." Elena's voice greeted her from above. "Here I am again."

Pidge trudged up the flight.

"Hmm, I see that." She landed in the room.

Her sister was sitting on a three-legged wooden stool and rummaging through a box of vintage knick-knacks. Dark, rich light from the hanging bulb reflected off the sprinkling of heirlooms throughout the room and off the wood floor.

Pidge leaned against the doorjamb. She sensed trouble. Her sister was crying out for help, carrying a manner of repression. Was she bordering on another bout of depression and insecurity?

She hoped this time she had all the answers her sister needed to hear and to arrange for conversion.

However, she had to be careful as she was extremely conscientious and took every criticism to heart. That was her delicate defense. Right now, Pidge needed a recruit. Maybe even a total support group.

She spied the flute sitting upright in a far corner. "Was that *you* I heard playing?" She sneezed from the dust.

"Yes." Elena straightened and fixed her gaze on her sister. "I hope I didn't disturb the neighbors, ha!"

"It sounded lovely." Her elevated response seemed to crack in the room. She sauntered over to inspect the collection in the box Elena was poking through. "Isn't it getting a little late in the day to be searching for things?" She realized her tight tone could have been friendlier, but she had every intention of spending a quiet evening with Bill, watching their favorite television shows. Maybe her sister wouldn't be at this too much longer.

"I suppose." She showed her a green porcelain ashtray. "Dad's, remember? He'd come home from a long day selling appliances and light up his big 'ole cigar."

"Yep." She crossed her arms. "Joseph Polson was a family man, always making sure we were fed, clothed, and secure."

He was also a man who was unapproachable and distant. Always at arm's length, he wasn't exactly uncaring, but selective in his affection nonetheless. There was never a time when either girl shared the same closeness with him as they had with their mother.

Sadly, the image of him eluded her these days.

A flash of reminiscence dwelled in Elena's eyes. "That he did. I can still sometimes smell that nasty old thing." She stroked the pottery with affection.

They both snickered.

"Anyway, I just didn't want to work today. Hunt's at a meeting, and I was lonely." She wrapped the ashtray with its newspaper protection and put it back into the box.

"Sweetheart, you're procrastinating. It's not like you." She slanted a glance at her, pressing for more information. "Do you have writer's block, or depression?" She nestled into the rocker and smoothed down her lemon-yellow bohemian-style skirt.

Elena sighed. "Not sure. It's like all my emotions are conspiring against me." There was urgency in her voice. "I can't seem to shake the feeling." She closed the flaps on the box and hunched over it. "What can I do about it, Pidge? Coming here, I feel like a fish surfacing for fresh air." She carried a take-me-away look on her face, a look there should be a law against.

"Ah, I hate to tell you, but the air in here is far from fresh." She giggled.

A shadow slipped out of the corner and gave the impression of coming to life.

"You know what I mean." Elena straightened and clasped her hands. "When I pass through these doors, I feel transformed, humble. Like a restoration drapes over me."

It was as if she was dreaming out loud. The way her eyes lit up, they might as well have been witnessing a revelation. Was she quoting some of her writing? Pidge couldn't tell. She decided to lend a more sympathetic ear.

"My, you do have a way with words, I'll grant you that. No wonder you're in the career that you are."

"It comes with the territory." She stood and stretched her back.

A silence dominated the stagnant space.

"My nerves are wearing down with the kids," Elena admitted. "Sometimes I can't count on Hunt to be there for discipline."

A current of May wind grew its power against the window.

"I'm limited on how far I can take authority." She replaced the box in its proper home on a shelf in the far corner.

"The way I see it," Pidge said, "you must really love him to sacrifice for his grandkids." She rocked in place.

"I do, Pidge. I really do. He works so hard for all of us." She played with a strand of hair. "Neither one of us knows what exactly to do. Sometimes he gets so over-the-top exasperated."

"I can imagine." It wasn't often Pidge put the man on a pedestal. In fact, she didn't hold high regard for him. As far as she was concerned, he drank way too much and often neglected her sister's welfare. However, she could sympathize on those bratty teenagers. They were high maintenance. She hoped Hunt wasn't just using Elena to watch over them when he couldn't.

She'd seen it happen in other relationships.

Fortunately, Elena could hold her own. Even with her other issues, she'd never been one to be dependent.

"Needless to say, it's getting too much for me to handle, Pidge." She rubbed her hands together, a hint of anxiety in her words.

Pidge Morton took on the role of liaison between her sister and Hunt Klyce. Why couldn't Elena confide in her boyfriend the way she could in her? "Good lord, you do have it bad." She stopped the rocking action and twisted her lips.

"Ever feel like a rundown house needing tender loving care? With no dreams left?" Elena tilted her head and raised her eyebrows, angling for assurance.

"Not lately." She shifted, afraid her thigh muscle might cramp. "So you've been scratched, but not scarred. Big deal. Who hasn't?" She bowed her head and toyed with recollections of her own, remembering all the rejections from men she received while she was in the dating phase. The process had been mortifying. Thank goodness Bill Morton had come along when he had to boost her ego, which had been at an all-time low. "Besides, my dear, dreams know no boundaries."

"Oh, I love that! I'll make a mental note of that quotation and use it in one of my campaigns." She laughed, tapping her temple. "Thank you, sis."

Pidge clasped her left wrist with her right fingers. "Yeah, I heard that on one of the talk shows. *Ellen, The View . . .*" She closed her eyes to remember. ". . .maybe it was *Dr. Phil*. Sounds like something he would come up with."

Elena peered out the window. It supplied a southern exposure.

"Dearest," Pidge continued, "you have obligations now. I realize you aren't used to them, you're used to being free as a bird." She rested her elbows on her knees, hoping the wisdom penetrated. "But your life has changed. The rules have changed. And . . . you have to speak up to be heard." She didn't want the words to come across as insulting or callous.

Elena drew in a deep breath and squinted from the contrasting light.

"And you have to own up to the responsibilities," she said, offering more input. Somewhere, somehow, she'd gotten a second wind. "That is, if you want to. Volunteers weren't born, they're made." The extent of her insight only reached so far. Mental exhaustion began to set in.

"Thank you for your honesty." Elena turned and glided over to her sister, resting a hand on her shoulder.

"Hey, I *am* honest . . . but I'll stretch the truth when needed."

"Like now?"

"No, sweetheart. Not now."

The familiar red cardinal flew onto the windowsill and called out to another feathered friend.

"There's going to come a time when you have to make a decision. For your own sake," Pidge insisted. "Only you can do what must be done in your life. You, and no one else. Not even me." She felt weariness journeying through her system. The day was stretching beyond her limits. "You have to do what's necessary."

The bird pecked at the glass.

"If only I could do an ultrasound on my soul. I wonder what it would show?" Elena sat back down on the stool. "The kids and I will never be on the same page. I don't know how to delve out conditions, I'm too lenient. They don't take me seriously." Her shoulders slumped as she inspected the floor. "I'm so tired of being diplomatic, of being the bad guy. It's as if I'm living two lives at once. The generation gap is way too wide."

Pidge raised her chin. "From what I understand, what parent of a teenager *does* know what it takes? I've never had the pleasure, so I'm useless in advice. I sit in your corner in the select group of childfree women." At this point in their lives, both sisters should be biological grandparents. But it takes having children to reach that status. "If they can't take your serious motives as gospel, then I don't know what to tell you." Pidge didn't want her sister to just be a shadow of a woman, lost in a fog. From observation, these Klyce kids definitely took advantage of her.

"And I need an excessive use of say-so, but I can't seem to get it." Elena coughed. "If I had my own child in this day and age I wouldn't know which way to turn. Dr. Spock is long gone, and so is his advice." She played with the hem of her jeans. "Besides, it wouldn't work now anyway."

"I agree!" The words came out swift, not punctual.

"At fifty-four, my chances are as near zero as one could get. My opportunity has come and gone." Wetness ringed her eyes. "Although Janet Jackson just had a baby at fifty," she speculated, brightening.

"Maybe it's a good thing your chances are gone. But I certainly would've helped if you'd had one." She worked her way out of the seat. It was time to end this. "Sweetheart, you need to take a break. Find some kind of outlet." She did, too, but didn't add the thought to the conversation. Lately, she had taken up crocheting, but it wasn't giving her much pleasure. She needed to find another hobby.

"Pidge, we weren't raised in a household with liberties or punishments. We were too good, remember?" She stood, installing her hands in her front pockets. "But these kids? Their manners have a lot left to be desired. I try to keep an open mind, but when that's not possible, that's when I get frustrated. I figure my expectations are too damn high." The words urged foresight.

"We've all had to make sacrifices. But you . . ." Pidge hesitated and pointed at Elena. ". . .you've been more courageous in your choices."

The point was made clear.

"Should I take that as a compliment?"

"Naturally." Pidge wandered over to the hanging light. "They're teenagers, sweetheart. The trouble is today they all have too many choices."

She switched off the light, and descending daylight took over the illumination. "Besides, when we know too much, it takes the fun out of life. Don't you agree?"

A small snicker escaped Elena`s lips. "I suppose." Merriment shone in her hazel eyes. For an instant, they resembled two shamrocks concealed under glass.

Pidge spotted a neglected cookbook and retrieved it. "Hey, check this out." She leafed through the yellowed pages. "Anything you might be able to use?" The musty aroma from her mother's cooking almost reverberated off the pages.

"One of Mom`s," Elena noted, touching a page. "They were like bibles to her." She let loose a grin. "Remember the magazines she used to buy? *Good Housekeeping, Better Homes and Gardens, American Home*—they were full of recipes, good advice, things that would soon lose their influence." Her face registered perseverance. "I'd like to think some things haven't changed."

"Yeah. With the way she cooked, how come we used to weigh so much less?"

Elena inspected her own outfit of tight pants and a turquoise crewneck sweater. "Beats me! And remember? She would never even think about using paper plates or utensils. Nothing artificial."

"Oh, heavens no!" She sneezed. "Most of the time we were growing up, we didn't even have things like that."

A unified chuckle took the tension away.

The exhaust from the teakettle whistled up the stairs. "Join me for tea?" Pidge asked.

"Absolutely." Her agreeable smile held merit.

Pidge gave Elena the book and they closed the door on the attic behind them.

The cleaner air that greeted them was more than welcomed.

TEA TIME

Elena followed Pidge downstairs and through the Morton household, passing the standard fare of antiques that hinted of past prosperity.

In the kitchen, Pidge poured the hot water into porcelain China teacups, heirlooms from their paternal grandmother. The sisters took their cups and matching saucers and settled at the dining table, selecting their tea bags from a vintage Fiesta canister. At the far end of the room, their mother's oak buffet stood guard while a hearty aloe vera plant loomed atop it.

Pidge squeezed into the narrow space between the table and the wall with difficulty, dropping her body heavily on one of the vacant ladder-back chairs. She occupied every square inch of the space.

As the liquid cooled in their cups, Elena and Pidge continued their conversation from the attic.

"This belongs to us and nobody can take it away." Pidge said, referring to the house. She raised her cup toward Elena in a toast as the steam fogged her eyeglasses. Behind them, her brown eyes, round with something enduringly surprised and hurt in their expression, remained youthful in spite of the network of lines beneath them.

Elena dabbed her teabag into the water. "I can still see Mom in here, fixing our meals and baking cookies with her tin cutters."

"Which I still have," Pidge said with affection.

"I know. Those raisin oatmeal cookies were to die for!"

"I have to agree." She rested her chin on a free hand.

"Remember all the holiday feasts that came out of this room?" Elena felt herself relax. "Sometimes I can still smell them."

Pidge blew across her cup in an effort to cool the liquid. "Yes. And in her quiet ways, she was always dressed prim and proper, even with jewelry."

"Nothing has compared since," Elena said, crossing her arms. "Those were the days: dairy delivery, bottled soda, penny candy, five and dimes— all before the dreaded Walmart." She hesitated with thought. "And cruising in the back seat of Dad's Chrysler Imperial. Without seat belts, I might add."

The trip down memory lane brought smiles to the women's faces.

"And Mom would even send us with a list to the corner grocery store, when we were old enough not to have to worry about our safety or someone's perversion," Elena added.

Pidge nodded. "And she knew where we were every minute."

"'Tis true." She blinked heavily, lifting the teacup for another toast. "To sisterhood."

Pidge mimicked the gesture. "Amen." She took another sip of the hot liquid.

"We promised Mom that, remember?" Elena couldn't help spreading her smile. "That we'd always be here for each other. We're bonded." The tea was warm on her throat.

"Forever."

With cup in hand, Elena slipped out of the chair, never one to sit long. She leaned against the cool sink counter. A blend of the green tea and the morning's bacon aftermath cruised through the air. "Aren't we blessed to remember the simple things?" She tilted her head. "Like playing board games, going downtown to window shop, being measured for new shoes?"

Pidge adjusted her bra strap. "Goodness, you're on a roll. I particularly loved going on roadside picnics and to Grandma's every Sunday . . . ." She paused in contemplation. "Even dressing up our dolls."

"Absolutely!" Elena nodded, taking a healthy swig of the brew. "Before recycling, cable, and satellite—even the women's movement."

"Hear! Hear!"

Outside, a light rain began to fall and the sky darkened.

"Oh, Pidge, I wanna go back. Go back to when things made sense." She siphoned the thought as though she were drinking it through a straw. "Be

Britni's age again. When things were simple, normal. Why can't that life work now?"

"Because, dear, time doesn't stand still."

"I feel a responsibility to keep memories alive. If I don't, who will?" She focused on a far corner of the room. "Even if I had a family today, how could I continue those traditions we just talked about in this crazy, mixed-up world we live in?"

Pidge fixed her hair behind one ear. "I get it. I truly do. It's not easy getting older." She shook her head with expertness and knowledge. "Believe me!"

"Yeah, but I don't want it to flash by either. Or have those images elude me." The ticking of the wall clock was the only sound to momentarily penetrate. "I just need to get a second wind—or third, or fourth. Right now, I'm just coasting along. Off base." She scratched her forehead.

"Ha! Who isn't?"

Is there an underlying implication to that statement? Elena wondered. *With my own dilemma, have I missed some subtle clues from Pidge?* Knowing her sister, she surely would have mentioned something by now, would have let Elena know if things weren't on the level.

"I just need to feel something new—spanking new," Elena said. "I'm so tired lately. Tired of the same humdrum." She let her face fall. "Any ideas?" She studied Pidge's expression for any hidden clues of strife, but none were present.

Her sister took a few minutes to ponder before answering. "What about going on a cruise? You've never done that." She stroked the edge of the table as if she petted a cat.

"Hmm . . ." She leaned forward. "As long as it's one for singles." The white vinyl floor received a definite workout from her treading.

Pidge stared at her. "You know you don't mean that. How about finding a peaceful mountain retreat? Take a break and replenish."

Elena fingered the window of the back door, tracing the raindrops on the other side of the glass. "Sounds good, except the part where I'd have to come back," she teased. "Oh, Pidge, I'd love to do things I used to. Roller or ice skating." Elena twisted her lips, turning to amble back to the counter. "Or even going forty miles over the speed limit on a deserted road!"

"Then what's stopping you?"

"Lots. Hey, what about dancing? Yeah. I need to dance for hours and hours! Step up my regular workouts." She mock-curtsied. "Hunt doesn't dance, you know."

Pidge appeared to stay noncommittal on that tidbit.

Elena continued her spiel. "How about riding a roller coaster ten times in a row? Or even white-water rafting? Whad'ya say?" She invested in a wide grin.

"Sounds like you have a lot of regrets." Pidge yawned. "Or haven't had enough wild times. One or the other."

"True, it's not that I have many regrets, it's just that the ones I have are major." Her self-pity was in the bloating stage. "Sometimes I just have to look in the mirror in order to really see my life."

The neighbor's cocker spaniel started a barking tirade.

"We can't always help what we do, dearest, the decisions we make. Some just come naturally." Pidge smoothed the tablecloth with her hand. "And our options have begun to narrow with age." An apprehensive expression lit up her face. "Add to that, the laughs and inspirations just keep getting harder to find."

At that moment, Elena once again appreciated her only sibling's sincere, uncomplicated, and sweet nature. She counted Pidge as one of her treasured blessings, the permanent shoulder she could lean on, the hug-therapy she oftentimes needed. She had a knack of setting her on the path to objectivity. She was her compass, her beneficiary of wisdom.

Elena tapped her fingers under the counter's edge. "I get it, I really do. But I'm just out of my element. I don't fit in. You know, kinda like a misfit," she said. "My common sense has gone into overload. I feel like I'm dancing without music, or even that I'm the B-side of those 45 records upstairs." She pointed her chin to the ceiling. "I feel like I'm at the lip of a cliff—one false move and over I go . . . I just don't want to become a bitter middle-aged woman striving to make both ends meet."

The landline phone rang but quickly turned silent.

"Oh no, not again!" Pidge said. "We've been getting these crank calls."

"Really?" She reseated herself. "What a shame." Maybe this was the reason behind Pidge's unspoken concern.

Pidge raised her eyebrows. "Now there's an idea for your work. Hang-up calls, and how they affect the person answering."

Elena chuckled. "I'll keep it in mind. Try to give it some kind of angle." She sighed. "At present I'm as empty of ideas for promotions as a squeezed orange is of juice."

Pidge snickered and rubbed her neck.

"There are times when I wonder if anyone cares what I have to say anyway. When I wonder what my copywriting really means." Recently, she'd figured that in the face of disappointment, of continually giving her best and trying to make it better, all were fruitless. "Besides, what or who is better because of me and my creative life?" She was in a slump and had best find her way out. The kids were only partly to blame.

"Me, silly!" Pidge drew in a breath of patience. "And those customers who answer those ads. Perhaps it's the fact that you have a solitary career with no social life. Do you think?"

"You could be right," Elena said. "Sometimes I feel like I'm in an abyss with no way out." She could use more friends than the few leftovers from her previous fifteen-year-old radio stint who she wasn't all that close with. When they did get together, the small circle seemed to keep conversations on a professional level.

Stillness soon captured the air.

"My only true claims to fame are a few successful ad campaigns and being a future step-grandmother, if I choose to stay the course." She allowed skepticism to sneak into her voice. "I'm like an ordinary coin in circulation and everybody's looking for a rare one." She chortled. "Better yet, an old chair needing to be reupholstered."

"Hey, there are worse lives." Pidge seemed ready to end the conversation.

Elena realized the hour grew late. "I suppose." She drew in an extended breath. "I do know one thing for certain. Every time after I leave here"—she twisted a strand of hair between two fingers—"I can go home or to the office and produce up a storm. But when it comes to freeing my own emotions, I can't seem to achieve the same feeling."

"Oh, dear." Pidge took a moment for reflection, contorting her face. "Maybe . . ."

"Yes?"

"Maybe you should set up your business here." She straightened. "Yes, here. Up in the attic."

"Excuse me?" Elena listened attentively, her eyes wide.

Both women allowed a period of silence.

"Yeah." Pidge bent her eyebrows into high arches. "Perhaps that would solve your problem. Your flow of creativity, at least."

Now and then, Pidge displayed remarkable flashes of insight that her sister could use a dose of.

Elena rose and paced back and forth again, as if she waited on a late ride. "Are you serious? What a wonderful idea!" She fixed her gaze on Pidge. "Could I? Could I really?"

A revived glow displayed itself on Pidge's face. "Well, of course I'll have to run it by Bill. And you'd have to do a helluva renovation job." She clasped her hands in front of her on the table. "In its present state, it's much too dreary. Plus, you'd have to add an outside stairway."

Elena also contemplated the possibilities. "I never even thought of it." In her mind's eye, she visualized a bright transformation of the cherished room. "The attic just has a way of settling my soul. When I'm up there, it's as if I've come full circle. Even though I'm a square!"

Another round of laughter filled the air.

"Good. It's decided then." Pidge jerked herself free from her chair and took the dishes to the empty sink.

"I have so much to do, so much to organize." Elena fake-clapped at chest level. "Do you honestly think Bill will let me use the attic?" She peered over Pidge's shoulder with a newfound resolve.

"I do, and it *would* be convenient, now that I really think about." They lived less than seven easy miles from each other. "And I hope it's a step in the right direction for you." She faced Elena and drew her in for a hug.

"And the kids will be on summer break at their dad's soon, so I'll have lots of quality time to spend on it." She paused. "I love you so much! I'm so lucky to have the best sister in the world!"

The rain had departed, yet clouds still closed up the sky.

"I feel the same way. And I'm grateful you come to me when you have to talk to someone." She smiled at Elena at arm's length.

"You'll never know how much I appreciate your being here for me." She took the moment to heart. "I don't know what I'd do without you." She pulled back the responsive curtain to reveal courage.

Inhale.

Hold.
Exhale.
Calm.
Safe.

She found her purse and tucked it under her arm. "But right now, I should be going. I just realized I left my phone in the car and I'd better check it." She placed a hand on Pidge's shoulder. "Thanks for letting me vent." She licked her lips. "And for the wonderful suggestion. Maybe it's what I need."

"Any time." Pidge walked her to the back door.

The phone rang again, interrupting their farewell.

All of a sudden, Elena's instinct kicked in. She felt that something wasn't right. Similar to the time she received the call about her mother's death.

"Hold on," Pidge instructed her as she went and answered the phone. "Oh, dear," she said into the receiver as she shot Elena a look full of dread, then offered the handset to her. "It's Hunt."

The room became eerily quiet as Elena made her way to the wall unit.

"Hi." She breathed heavily into the mouthpiece. "What's up?"

When she heard his words, her heart skipped a beat as shock became sole owner of her emotions.

Pidge stroked the nape of her neck when Elena handed back the phone.

"It's Decker. He's in jail." Weakness gripped and took possession. She felt as if she were in a coal mine that had just caved in.

If it hadn't been for the stove being where it was in the kitchen and breaking her fall, Elena would have injured herself when she fainted.

DO DOGS GO TO HEAVEN?

Decker Klyce was barricaded in the county jail's holding area. His 170-pound frame, full of reluctance, lay on the unforgiving platform bed. The dim walls and ceiling closed in on him. Not to mention the stale odor of urine.

He rubbed his wet brown eyes and spent some time with his conscience. Time that a price tag couldn't be put on. This was the perfect opportunity to end the game he found himself in, to terminate the insanity. To go find Scribes and square things. To cry out to his mother or father or grandfather that he was sorry.

The charade had caught up with him. And now he was behind bars late on a Saturday night, awaiting his fate, chilled to the bone.

He suddenly knew what those dogs he and Scribes abused must have felt like. Abandoned, with little hope. Sad. Lost.

Throughout the night, the authorities had questioned him for what seemed like an eternity. He'd denied any allegations, tired beyond belief. They were letting him temporarily sleep off the guilt. At least he hadn't been strip-searched. That would have been degrading.

Would his dad, or granddad, save him? He realized he had a lot to lose. Certainly his youth.

Not to mention freedom and what little self-esteem he had left.

When he got out of this lockup, he must figure out some plan to keep away from the bad influence of the guy he was terrified of. With his mounting fear of Scribes Cantrell, Decker had kept his mouth shut up to now.

That would have to change or he'd face more than a sentence.

He rose and lumbered over to the cold vertical steel bars. He slipped his forearms into the free spaces between, wishing the rest of his body could follow suit. But he was trapped, in more situations than one. He detected another inmate screaming out profanities down the line.

A stiff middle-aged guard with a menacing demeanor suddenly appeared. He made the same expression as Andrew Jackson on the twenty-dollar bill. "Can I help you?"

"When can I get outta here?" Decker put urgency in his voice.

"Soon's someone gets ya out." With that, he turned his back and stalked away in his squeaky boots.

If only Decker could do the same.

Resuming his position on the thin mattress, he folded his hands behind his head. The taste of the cold eggs they'd served him hours ago still roamed around his mouth. Afterward, he'd regurgitated them but didn't fully vomit, leaving a vinegary taste in his mouth.

He had to get out of this place!

But how?

He thought back to tonight's episode.

As usual, he'd been very cautious sneaking out the window after everyone else in the house fell asleep. It made him feel grown up, yet unnerved just the same.

Meeting up at their designated spot at midnight, the boys had hunched at the railing's side, waiting for just the right car. The May night air had been heavy with a coming fog.

Scribes had selected the vehicle below them on the thoroughfare. He always did well with that assignment. Besides, Decker wasn't inclined to take charge; courage was in short supply in his system.

The dead Irish Setter had lain between them. When Decker briefly recalled the moment, he felt a pang of contempt toward his friend. The animal was no doubt a family pet, a loyal member of some household. He had asked himself silently how he'd feel if something happened to a beloved companion, if he were to have one.

However, he never belabored the sentimentality. If he had, they wouldn't have been waiting to pull their stunt.

"Here it comes. The one." Scribes had a knack of talking as if he had too many teeth.

Decker had taken the dog's front feet, Scribes the rear. The action had been rehearsed many times.

"One . . . two . . ." The car had approached with perfect timing.

"Three!"

The dog had gone over the side, into the windshield. Discarded like a bag of garbage.

No consideration was given to results or penalties in the moment.

Many times, however, Decker had wondered if they were breaking the law . . . or just bending it.

They had automatically sprinted from the scene, dashing into the woods in separate directions. Despite the weight they carried on their plump frames, they could have qualified for the Olympics in the one-hundred-meter dash.

No one would ever guess who they were. Or why they did it.

Why did they do it? Decker often wondered. Scribes had never fully explained his reasons, just said that it was a form of excitement. A way to get on the news anonymously.

How else would they be acknowledged?

Scribes's home life didn't provide any stability, Decker knew that for sure. His callous father showed no respect to any of his family members. He couldn't care less about their lives. Without any attention on the home front, the boy searched it out by other means. That's the one thing he and Decker had in common.

Ever the bully, Scribes was determined to get notice somewhere. He'd make sure it happened.

When they'd met up at their follow-up location a half mile in the distance, Decker had been out of breath, on edge. "We did it!" His jangled nerves had played host to timidity. He had a feeling this time was different.

How right he had been.

"I love scarin' people like that!" Scribes had caught his breath and was walking as if he strolled on thin ice. In fact, there had been a hint of swagger in his step while his shoulders betrayed a victorious lift. "Ain't it fuckin' great?" His unflinching voice had choked with nervous laughter. "Just how we planned it."

You'd think they were talking about a school competition the team had just won.

"Awesome." Decker had concealed a smirk. His throat had been sore from the night's air, like when he used to scream on the playground during recess. Not that long ago.

These days, he was into grown-up things, adult games.

He associated his deeds with the feeling he had the first time he opened a gift without adult supervision. Glorious!

He loved the arena, although he was still trying to conquer his mental inhibitions. His dad had once said, "If you don't like the stakes, you'd better not play."

He had yet to figure out that advice.

Decker now lay on his right side, facing the cell's cement-block wall. He blinked back the tears lying in wait as his emotions scattered. "Oh, Dad. Where are you now?" The words were loud enough to echo throughout the confined space, one with no privacy even though he had no cellmate.

Within minutes, he returned to the memory.

"Keep in mind, not one word to anybody," Scribes had warned. The humor had gone out of his voice by that point, stolen by the state of affairs. "Got it?" He'd squared his shoulders while his liquid-dark eyes gave notice. The words were repeated each time they performed the ritual, ever suggesting a threat. The guy carried around a volatile attitude as if it were a first-place trophy he had won in a soapbox derby.

A response had swum around Decker's brain but wouldn't come out.

"Well?" Scribes had raged.

"No problem," Decker had obliged with the intensity of promise. He remembered biting his bottom lip, not realizing how hard he was doing it until he tasted the sickish sweetness of blood. "You've got my guarantee." As a result, a hint of pride proved authentic.

Shortly after, the boys had parted ways.

Now drawing imaginary stick figures on the textured wall, Decker thought about how he hadn't noticed Scribe's impulsive nature until recently. Had he been that infatuated with the guy's temperament? It was calculating, and harmful. Eaten up with ambition—albeit the wrong kind—he was an accident just waiting to happen.

The guy sneered even when enjoying himself. He was like a false alarm ready to cause unnecessary panic. The type of person who would steal a blanket off a shivering orphan. No one fit in his shadow.

No one would dare.

At present, Decker heard muffled voices and footsteps in the corridor. He stiffened, expecting any possibility or consequence. He knew both were in his immediate future.

Then, silence again.

There was no window to use as an indicator of light, and without any other way to tell time, he figured he'd been incarcerated for five hours.

He covered up with the thin sheet. The black T-shirt and torn jeans he wore didn't add any warmth.

He shouldn't be here, of all places.

Once again, his thoughts took over.

When he and Scribes had eventually palled around in the school cafeteria, it was because the ruffian had intimated him, sucking him right into his evil web. Decker was sure Scribes saw him as vulnerable, young, and although not exactly stupid, not altogether smart either. Why did he need a partner? He had a brother or two who could serve in that malicious role.

Perhaps he had guessed Decker wanted to be a part of something, a prime target who wanted a change-up in his life.

If so, Scribes had been correct in his calculations.

But now, they'd been caught. The gig was up.

He was on the inside looking out.

And Decker knew for certain that if he confessed, Scribes had a method of quieting him. He'd heard stories of how the guy would corner his victims and belittle them before inflicting bodily harm, with help from his big brothers. Reputation had it they relished the opportunity to physically threaten someone.

When would Decker Klyce ever figure out for himself that he was just one drop in a human wave of adolescence? That Scribes had only sought him out for a partner in crime? Nothing more.

He shivered under the surprisingly clean-smelling sheet, wondering if it was from his bleak circumstances or the temperature.

To counteract his anxiety and scattered emotions, he took a moment to proudly reflect on the final event resulting from his insightful sneaking skills.

Before tonight, he could always count on them, getting away with climbing in and out of his bedroom window every time. No one in the household even knew he was out and about at late hours.

It had given him the redemption he so needed at this point in his fragile life.

With his mom in her own incarceration, she was focused on her own path. Which didn't include him or Britni. He missed her to no end.

His biological father never had the time for quality connection. He was too busy, stretched to the limit with his new family and work responsibilities.

So, who really cared about him in the long run?

He hugged his knees tight for comfort and coughed from the holed-up stench. He couldn't wait to beg forgiveness and apologize to all who were involved. He was too young to start this kind of life.

Yes, he had grown to rely on the secret prowling talent, allowing it to become second nature. During this whole ordeal, he'd learned to give lying a good treatment too.

But what he hadn't counted on this time was the cops waiting for him outside in the bushes. He'd never made it back inside to his bedroom.

For all he knew, none of his family realized he was even missing.

He did know for certain that the authorities would have to contact his guardian.

He wasn't ready to face his grandfather. He'd never be ready, mostly because neither of them had been in this predicament before to be able to react with any kind of rationality.

In addition, Decker had yet to learn of the impending news.

In just under three hours, he would discover that their latest target out on the interstate was none other than his own father's wife.

UNDER PROTEST

At 8:26 a.m., the guard informed Decker he was being bailed out. He had only enough time to wonder who would do so before his grandfather appeared on the other side of the bars.

He timidly hunched his shoulders and slid his shaking body out from under the protection of the sheet.

"Let's go." Hunt's words were deep and direct, spoken through a tight jaw.

After making the necessary arrangements, they left the jail and headed home.

The silent ten-minute drive stretched into infinity. Decker couldn't wait to barricade himself in his bedroom, his sanctuary.

But as soon as Hunt pulled into the driveway, he finally spoke. "Get your butt in the living room, pronto!"

With ears ringing, Decker clenched his teeth and did as he was told. He hobbled into the house and sank into the couch, a much more comfortable space than the jail cot. A recent bacon-and-egg aroma hung in the air and elicited a growl in his stomach. He didn't realize how truly hungry he was until that moment.

Maybe Elena had saved him some breakfast. It would be like her to do that. At the moment, she hovered in the corner, looking edgy with her arms crossed. Her face seemed washed-out.

She had no right to add to this dilemma.

"Where were you last night?" Hunt interrogated with imposing authority as he paced the room.

Decker had never actually noticed before how tidy the room was. The wooden furniture's dust-free surfaces sparkled, in particular Elena's vintage hutch filled with antique glassware. And the beige cobblestone-patterned carpet still looked brand new, while the pecan color on the walls gave the space an uncluttered personality.

For some reason, at this very minute, he experienced an endearing sense of home.

He cracked his knuckles. "Here . . . I was here." He heard his own wobbly voice reverberate.

"Don't lie to me!" Hunt snarled. He stomped into the next room and fixed himself a whiskey and soda, early as it was.

The atmosphere reeked with tension. If Decker could ascribe a color to this scenario, it would be lava orange.

Hunt returned to his captive audience, launching into a lecture and a worthy performance. When he finished, he said, "Now, I'll ask again. Where were you at one o'clock this morning?"

"Asleep, in my room." Decker thumbed toward the hall as his pulse quickened.

His grandfather took a healthy swig. "Well, that's interesting. Because your friend Scribes said you were with him."

Out of the corner of his eye, Decker noticed Britni's head sticking out of her bedroom door.

Just great! Talk about being ganged up on.

"Well?" his grandfather said, pushing for an answer.

"I . . . I . . ." Forecasting, he grit his teeth and held shaking knees in place.

Hunt marched the floor with the glass that could almost be a permanent prop in his hand. "I'm waiting." He jutted his chin. "I'm not stupid, so don't try to be cute."

Elena stood rigid, dodging the interrogation. She peered down as if she were praying.

Maybe she was.

Decker cowered deeper into the cushions with crossed arms, his dejection so marked it required something extra.

"Then let me help you out." Hunt slammed down the drink on top of the television. Elena shot him a glare. "Someone called 9-1-1 and identified this Scribes from another time at the same location. The same time of night." The audio brutality continued. "And he noticed the same long coat as before."

As Decker shook his head, tears built up but stayed put.

"Your dear friend Scribes was picked up, too, and confessed. And . . . he blames you as the instigator."

A quick, pitiful laugh escaped from Decker's lips. "What?" Just knowing that Scribes was in jail gave him an uncomfortable jolt.

"Quite the joke, isn't it?"

The fail-proof plan was unraveling by the minute.

Yeah, right, Scribes! Everything will be all right. We'll never get caught. Wrong!

"Well, here's the spoiler." Hunt paused with intention. "Your own stepmother was your latest victim."

"What?" The words came from Britni. She bolted down the hallway and landed in the fray. "NO! What have you done?" Clearly shaken, her eyes were two pools of ice directed at her brother.

"Don't worry," Hunt said, now leaning against the doorjamb. His brows bumped together in a scowl. "She's okay. Lucky you."

The atmosphere seemed to relax for a short time.

"I had no idea." Decker gritted his teeth. "How could I have known?" His response was barely audible as he mentally argued with himself.

"Have we not impressed on you the fact that we are providing a home for you? That we expect some kind of respect? And this is the thanks we get?" He nodded in Elena's direction.

The only responses Hunt received were a retreat from Britni and continued sulking from Decker.

"I give up!"

Decker clasped his hands together tightly. "You're treating me like a child," he finally said, but his unapologetic statement didn't gain any points.

"You *are* a child! This isn't some kind of joke or prank." The air was again pregnant with hostility. It was as if all of them were waiting for a grenade to explode in front of them. "This is serious."

84

Decker had never seen him so upset, or heard his voice sound so unfamiliar. His delivery spewed forth with a tone of both contempt and exasperation.

Would he eventually slap him?

After all, he *was* pretty angry.

"I'm thirteen!" he retaliated, indignantly aware of the unsteadiness in his voice. "I'm almost grown up." His left leg bounced involuntarily and every line in his body expressed despair.

"Oh, geez whiz, a whole thirteen! But here I find myself babying the answers out of you." He marched again in front of the couch and he spread his hands in a gesture of mockery. "Does your age give you a right to kill dogs and hurt people?"

Decker supposed Hunt couldn't help the barrage of questions, but the outrage in his elder left him feeling nervous, unwelcome in his home. What if they threw him out? He had nowhere else to go.

"Grandpop, I'm sorry. But I wasn't the one who came up with this scheme." His speech dragged along much like the wounded animals he and Scribes had selected for their escapades. "I just stupidly went along with it."

The morning grew heavy with worry.

"Regardless, you could have killed your own father's wife! What were you thinking? Do you understand the consequences?" His habit of asking questions was too strong in the full-blown rampage.

Elena sat in the recliner. She must have abandoned any effort to partake in the conflict. Decker could sure use her neutrality at this point.

"I can't say anymore." He freed his shaking voice, knowing he sounded defensive. At the same time, a new, foreign rage against Scribes seized him in unknown proportions.

A thirty-second gap of silence added to the mix while a sudden chill crept through the room.

"So help me, if you're lying to me about all this, I'll make sure you don't have a social life for the next five years. I've already talked to the authorities and they let me take you home"—Hunt's face muscles hardened and his eyes narrowed—"for the time being."

"It's true. I was just an accomplice." Decker's appeal needed to add nine degrees of assertiveness to have any hope of calming his granddad. "And yes, I understand the consequences." He rubbed his forearm and swallowed with intention.

"Haven't you heard that a liar steals the truth?" Hunt said it as if it were a challenge and watched his grandson closely. "You've got a lot of nerve taking an animal's life. And almost a human one." His reprimand was magnified as he settled in beside Decker and caught his arm in a stranglehold. "My God!"

Decker waved the gesture, and the protest, away with white-knuckled fists. His jaws clamped and his head began to ache. As hard as he'd tried to keep his and Scribes's secret well hidden, he now had to live with the forthcoming repercussions from having this so-called friend.

His bravery and sarcasm were bottoming out while his emotions spiraled out of control. Oddly enough, for a brief moment he wanted to tell these grown-ups everything, but giving them the few fragments he possessed would serve no useful purpose.

"I said I was sorry. I'll call Dad later," he conceded.

Hunt finally acknowledged Decker's sincerity. "That's better."

The explanation having seemed to satisfy the adults, Elena broke into the discussion. "Let's all just lighten up now, all right?" On the verge of peace, she expressed the need to return to normalcy. "This is the kids' last week of school. And we just need to get through it, okay?" She didn't give Hunt a second to change his mind. "Does the finger have to point anywhere in particular? Seems there's a lot of blame being thrown around here."

Decker agreed with the idea in a hurry. At present, Elena wasn't so bad of a person. He stopped short of thinking she was a blessing to the family.

"No!" Hunt maliciously clipped the one word out. "This scandal could ruin me, ruin you," he said, addressing Elena. He made the point with cold and precise meaning. "There's a strong possibility we could be considered accomplices. No doubt it'll be in the News of Record in the newspaper." He ran his hands through his hair and turned toward Decker. "What they'll charge you with, I have no clue. A misdemeanor, I'm sure. Animal cruelty? Property damage? . . ." His words trailed off as his crimson face adopted more strain.

The too-evident attempt at solutions failed as Elena nodded in corroboration. Her intervention into the dialogue had been of little value.

"At best you'll get off with probation," Hunt predicted.

Decker realized everyone at school would know about this. Thank goodness he would have to endure the gossip for only a few days.

The silence grew thick as the scolding wore thin.

Decker unfolded himself like an extension ladder from the couch in which he'd been imprisoned. He sprang to his feet; his courage had run out. "Leave me alone," he muttered.

A change of scene would be most welcomed.

For all parties.

Hunt rose also and caught Decker's shoulder in his grip. "This isn't over by any means." The older man issued the ultimatum and turned away. "I can't believe all this." His speech dropped to a condescending note. "A juvenile delinquent for a grandson."

In the distance, one of their cell phones rang.

Decker took the opportunity to storm out. He slammed his bedroom door behind him so hard the house shook. Plopping down on his messy bed, he hid his head under the pillow and prayed, taking comfort in the fact that he was home.

At this point, he couldn't rule out the idea of running away. But where to?

He had no options and no financial means.

Even though he'd strayed far from the straight and narrow, he could sure use a hug right now. Or even a kind word.

One thing about it, at least after this he wouldn't have to tune in to the boring six o'clock news any longer. The press would concentrate on his crime only briefly, then be on to other developments.

A year from now, who would remember the incident, names, and outcome anyway?

By then, life would be different.

Fingers crossed he would never encounter Scribes again.

If only it were that simple.

WOULD YOU CARE FOR DESSERT?

Throughout the next few days, the turmoil lessened. One night, Elena played her flute on the couch while dinner cooked. The aroma of pot roast and peach cobbler teamed up in the air as she tried to get reacquainted with the notes and keys using a helpful musical chart she'd discovered on Google and printed out.

If only she could come across a chart to guide her everyday life with the Klyce family.

Hunt walked in the front door with one of his signature winks and a grin. "That sounds great, baby. And the house smells marvelous!"

"All for you," Elena replied, disassembling the flute and placing it back in its case. She joined him at the threshold and kissed him.

Tonight, she felt normal after all the woes. She attributed her fainting spell at Pidge's to too much stress all at once. Her sister had naturally been concerned, but Elena had regained consciousness only a few seconds afterward and convinced her it was just a one-time incident.

Hunt was still oblivious to the calamity. He had enough to worry about.

However, it was a wonder she hadn't had another one with the Decker episode.

"Why did you stop playing?" Hunt asked, gazing past her shoulder. "I rather liked what I heard."

She shook her head and shrugged. "You know how shy I am."

Standing back, she studied him as he slipped off his steel-toed boots. He wore a nervous, restless guise on his square face and bore a slightly harassed disposition, as if he were constantly being interrupted, or feared to be. When he'd confronted Decker about the criminal activity, Elena couldn't have begun to guess the outcome as she'd never seen him in that state. He had been beyond angry.

And rightly so.

The fiasco had been barely touched on since. It remained one of those cases where no news was good news. Yet all knew the probability of that would change soon. It was as if everyone involved was one step away from an encore of angst.

"You know," Hunt said, "this is one of my treasured times of the day. Looking forward to coming home to you and discussing our days over dinner." He stepped over to the recliner and eased into it, relaxing. His tan Oxford shirt was unbuttoned at the throat.

"With or without the kids?" She'd flung out the question before she could stop herself. She ran her hand through his tousled hair, knowing he'd raise a fuss if it needed to be combed. Hunt Klyce was very picky about his appearance.

"Without, silly." He glowered at her out of deep-set brilliant blue eyes but soon snuck in an addictive smile that always aimed to please. "This, and bedtime of course." He paused. "Just holding you right before we go to sleep."

He ignored her raised eyebrows.

"I like that answer."

She made her way into the kitchen to check on dinner. She had paired up sweet potatoes and carrots to complement the meat. Elena loved cooking for the man of her life, just like her mom had. She could remember Doretta spending more time in the kitchen than any other part of the house. In aprons, in patience, in success.

Smiling with delight, she smoothed down her pink polka-dot apron and recalled one particular day with her mother and sister when Pidge was eight, Elena five:

"Mommy, can we wear one of your aprons?" Pidge asked. Mrs. Polson was dressed in a black gingham one.

"I want the yellow!" Elena said. It was her favorite of the collection.

"Not me, I'm going to wear the white one." Pidge drew out the apron *from its designated drawer. "Yes, this one with the red pockets and all the flowers."*

After the girls put on the smocks, Doretta stood back and analyzed them with pleasure. "Well, if you two don't look like two peas in a pod." Her *joyful expression turned serious. "Promise me something?"*

Both girls stared at her.

"What, Mommy?" The words came out almost in unison.

"That you'll always be this close." Her speech seemed rehearsed. *"Carry on the love we feel in this house at this very moment."*

"We will!" The two sisters hugged.

Elena recollected how her mother's face had symbolized the simplicity of the era. The request had presented a lesson in nurturing. She returned to the present and to Hunt in the living room. His arms were crossed and he was listening to the local evening news on television. He seemed preoccupied. Home in body, but not in spirit.

"Everything okay?" she asked. "Rough day?"

"Yeah, I'm good. . . Why, oh why, did I choose this profession?" He spoke more to himself than to her. "Just because I loved to build things as a kid didn't exactly qualify me to become a project supervisor."

Elena stood behind him and rubbed his shoulders, cherishing their alone time. "What else would you be doing if not that?"

He hesitated. "Never thought about it. So I suppose it suits me."

She kissed the top of his head. "Exactly. No one has a perfect job."

"It just drains me some days."

"I know . . . I understand."

She glanced at the TV. None of today's broadcast mentioned the boys' arrests. Yesterday, the reporters had announced that two juveniles were responsible for the accidents and the authorities were waiting to press charges. She assumed it was all old news now.

"Ready to eat?" She came around from behind the chair and stood next to him.

He grabbed her hand and kissed it. "Absolutely."

Back in the kitchen, she placed all the fixings in chinaware and carried them to the tableclothed dining room table. She unhooked her apron and laid it on a nearby chair. No matter how much work was involved, she'd much rather eat at home than in a restaurant. And Hunt was on board with that also.

They sat simultaneously.

"This is fantastic, baby." He scratched his forehead. "You know it's one of my favorites."

"I do." She loved the peace and calm taking shape in the setting. "And thanks."

He had his own way of making her feel special and appreciated.

"So, how was your day?" he asked, buttering his potatoes. "Able to get that promotion done for the senior fair?"

The annual community event was six weeks away and the committee had consulted Elena a month ago for her expertise in contacting all the appropriate resources.

"The only thing I have left to do is touch base with the printing company." She took a sip of water. "After that, I'll have to distribute the flyers to strategic places. And hope it all comes together in the end." She tilted her head in consideration.

He waited a beat. "I'm so proud of you, my little entrepreneur." He raised his brows. "We all are."

All included the grandkids. Somehow their quality dinner conversations always gravitated toward Britni and Decker, who were at their paternal great-grandmother's for the evening. Next week, they would be off to their father's for the summer.

Hunt and Elena slipped into the familiar controversy of the kids, her work forgotten.

"I sure hope they are behaving themselves with Lyla," he said in between bites. "She doesn't need to know all their faults."

Elena snickered, finding it hard to avoid speculation.

They had both turned their minds away from the impossibility of Decker's impending sentencing. Each had mistaken the boy's actions for something else.

"Dammit, Decker can be intelligent and industrious when he wants to be. When he applies himself." He tugged at his left ear. "But the times when he's lazy and self-centered, I get so discouraged and—"

She interrupted the stream of his words as her fork stopped halfway to her plate. "Don't criticize yourself, you're doing the best you can under the

91

circumstances." Hunt Klyce's interior was pure sensitivity, his exterior suspicious. With her help, the utensil finished its journey.

He took a healthy sip of Jack Daniels. But the bottle wasn't emptying as quickly as in days of old.

Was he reforming?

Hope materialized.

Their relationship didn't qualify for Al-Anon or Alcoholics Anonymous. Hunt wasn't that far gone. Still, the disappointment was like a clinging vine.

Was she asking for too much too soon?

"I'd like to think I'm doing the best I can," he continued evenly. Without your help, I don't know what I'd do. I really appreciate everything you've done." He reached over, took her hand, and favored her with another of his stellar winks. "Truly."

The gesture caused a warm sensation to flow through her body. She had needed to hear those words. Life was great again.

Elena really did love him.

Right now, she was half satisfied, half inspired. Not a bad combination.

"Now I know why he was so focused on the local news," she admitted. "I had to wonder why a thirteen-year-old would be so interested in the evening broadcast."

He creased his brow. The room became so still a snowflake could be heard falling even though it was June.

"I suppose that did seem a little odd to you, didn't it, my love?"

She nodded. "And he was always talking to that Scribes. I had hoped they were just being teenagers, but I detected there was something more. Something just didn't seem right." She cocked her head.

"Oh, I think you were naturally overprotective, knowing you like I do."

"Maybe."

She had hated harboring any suspicions and so had given Decker the benefit of the doubt. But perception had soon been in danger of denial. "My gut instinct had told me he had more up his sleeve than his arm."

Hunt remained silent. Through the open window, they heard a horn honk down the street.

"It just bothers me that when you aren't here, I'm the bad guy." She drew in a deep breath. "And he can be conveniently deaf whenever I talk to him."

"I'll agree with you there." He twisted in his chair, drumming a handful of fingers on the table. "He could be a lot more than what he is." His passion for introspection showed through. "Sometimes there's not enough room for the chip on his shoulder."

"You sound like you're excusing his behavior away. He *does* have a wonderful personality when he chooses to display it. He's like a constant story, always full of surprises." She took a sip of water. "Especially with the arrest."

"I know." He fingered his plate and acquired a faraway look in his eyes.

The boy had messed with both of their minds. Would this be a pattern in years to come?

She took a bite of the stewed vegetables. "I don't condone all he does, but he seems to lead a detached existence, never volunteering any info. He always seems to be locked up in his bedroom."

He fixed his gaze on her.

"For instance, the other day I caught him on an erotic website. He accused me of sneaking around and spying on him." She crinkled her nose.

Hunt muffled a whistle. "Good Lord! Baby, I'm sorry."

"It's okay." She bowed her head. "We'll make it through."

A breeze blew in from outside and the air suddenly freshened with the potent scent of a lilac bush nestled under the open window.

"Ready for dessert?" she asked.

"I am, indeed."

She gathered the dishes alone this time, insisting he remain seated. He always helped clean up, but tonight he seemed especially tired. She returned with smaller plates and served up the gluten-free cobbler.

She reseated herself with a sigh. It was time to put Britni up for discussion.

"Now, your granddaughter's another story," she started. "She definitely has a great capacity for being stubborn. It's almost like a prerequisite."

He narrowed his eyes. "She comes honestly by it, getting that trait from her mother." He pointed with his fork to the pastry. "My, this is really good."

"Mmm . . . yes, it is. It's a new recipe I tried from a healthy alternative group on Facebook."

A moment of polite stillness passed.

"And Britni's need for independence causes me more than enough anxiety." She tightened her lips. "She has no time for any advice or guidance, that's for sure. Because when I interfere, it seems to be a candid battle."

His mouth formed an *O* but he made no comment.

"Well, your ex should be happy the girl followed in her footsteps of being a cheerleader," she said.

He grinned at the comparison. "I don't know about that."

"Did you ever think you would end up with a bookworm?" she ventured, finishing the last crumbs of the dessert.

He answered abruptly. "Never thought about it." He slid the plate to the center of the table. "Do I regret being with a studious, beautiful woman? Hell, no!"

A chill crept through her. "Do you think your grandkids are ashamed of me?"

A look of surprise skipped across his face. "What? Heavens no! Why would you ask something like that?"

"Had I been someone else with more . . . with more pizzazz, would they have done better with the adjustment?"

His stare rested on her. "Stop that! Would it help you to know that I've decided I'm going to have a talk with both of them? Sit them down when they get back and explain a few things, whether they like it or not." He folded his hands on the table. "This is still our house and we have rules."

Between this news and Pidge's offer of the attic, which she had yet to discuss with him, she welcomed redemption. "Oh, Hunt, that would be great." She heard a solemn tone in her voice.

Could she believe him? Trust him?

Would the kids be more tolerant of her afterwards?

He got up and disappeared into the kitchen, returning with a bottle of Zinfandel and two wine goblets.

"Now, quit all this nonsense about not being good enough." He poured the wine with finesse. "I love you and there's no need to wonder otherwise." He sat back down and offered her a toast. "You know you stole my soul when I first saw you. In fact, I'm not sure I could breathe without you now."

Did Elena still have possession of her soul? Or had she given it to him in return?

94

They drank in sync while an affectionate regard passed between them.

"The first time I saw you, I knew we had something special between us," he said.

"Admit it, you were infatuated, not in love," she teased, pointing at him.

"Wrong! You always thought that, but I was in love with you from day one." He topped off her goblet.

"Oh, Hunt, you're so full of it." She made the words light and playful. It was good to laugh again. She'd almost forgotten how.

He tilted up his chin. "I used to watch you leave Paddy's, wishing I could go with you." His eyes conserved tenderness. "When we'd meet there on the sly."

Elena had heard the story before. Was it just a line, or was he sincere?

"And I tried to tell myself that what I saw was what I'd get," he said. "But you were so much more than that."

She remembered how he'd taken her by surprise. Back then, she'd been ready for another relationship, and he was ready to get out of his marriage. So, the timing had been perfect.

Right?

"Furthermore, you could be very persuasive," he said passionately. "You were, after all, my favorite sin." He sipped the wine.

They both took a moment to relive the memories.

"Do you recall the time when we first hooked up and you said, 'I won't be married by year's end?'" she said, trying to tantalize him with exaggerated carelessness.

"How could I forget? You called it my sales pitch."

At the time, she'd given him an ultimatum after five months of the affair: get a divorce or she was moving on. Like a gentleman, he had accepted the marching orders with dubious pride.

But in time, he couldn't stand to be without her and he contacted an attorney.

Neither was to blame. Each had a share in the dilemma, even Gwen. She had physically let herself go, not caring any longer about her outward appearance.

"You became a habit I didn't want to break. I won't say you were a bad one, just a habit." He flashed her one of his should've-been-a-huckster-in-a-previous-life expressions.

Hunt Klyce could be so sweet. Since she'd known him, she had counted on him to right the wrongs of her life. At present, some of those injustices still existed.

Like the alcohol. Why did he have to drink so much? Or was it something more? She couldn't think of any good answers. But she knew for certain that with everything else going on, it didn't help.

Sometimes, she felt as though she couldn't be extended credit because of her emotional debts.

"Oddly, I wanted to arrest you for being a chronic remedy to all of my problems at the time," he said, taking another swig.

Yeah, and you should be arrested for public intoxication.

Stop it, Elena! Treasure this moment!

She wanted to maintain her good mood. It had been a while since they'd been in hospitable territory, so she put any negativity about his alcohol consumption aside for the moment.

"We were destined to be together. We are those soul mates people talk about." His voice cracked with emotion, and with small slurs.

She couldn't agree more. She prayed his words would work, that she could just settle down and accept the permanency of this relationship.

Why put her security at risk?

Maybe she simply didn't recognize the feeling. In the end, she didn't have much experience with commitment. Every time she had gotten close to a man, he had either backed off or left. Two short young marriages were proof of that. However, not to be ignored was the common denominator of herself.

With utmost surprise, Hunt Klyce was different.

He had staying power.

Perhaps it was because he'd been down that family road of detours and exits and come out intact. And she needed that strength lacking in her own persona.

"You *do* know you complete me. You balance out my life." Hunt's philosophy gained big points with her. "We're necessary for each other; we couldn't do without one another."

She gauged an appropriate response. "Then no explanation is needed, I can't argue with that." She rose to clear the table, and at the same time the gurgling of a small plane's engine passing over invaded the room.

As she collected the dishes, she assembled her thoughts. The grandkids came to the forefront of her mind again. Their appearance onto the scene was another story altogether.

They hadn't been an easy adjustment. When Hunt had discussed getting part-time custody due to his daughter's condition, Elena's reluctance rushed to the forefront. She had been childfree and independent all her adult life, had never even been seriously involved with a man with children, let alone grandchildren. How could she know the effects would prove more than a challenge?

Should she have moved on then? Moved on to where? Had her choice let her down?

She felt similar to a clock that had idled. Stymied.

Working about in the kitchen, she started the dishwater and felt like shouting out "Life's gotten in the way around here." But she'd used up all her conversation. And there was no point in risking confrontation. The evening had been upbeat.

Wiping off the counter, she drew circles with the towel. The action reminded her of all the obstacles swirling around without mention. When she stopped, she realized she wanted to be in control again. Of what, she wasn't sure.

Elena had to make some kind of commitment before it was too late.

Breathe in.

Hold.

Breathe out.

Steady now.

EVERYBODY SAY "CHEESE"

The last twenty-one days rotated through Elena's mind as she drove to Yelden's Photography Studio on a bright July Saturday morning. The kids' dad was bringing them to meet her and Hunt at ten o'clock for a family portrait.

On June 14, Decker and Scribes had been officially arrested for the misdemeanors of destruction of property, cruelty to animals, and endangering lives. Decker confessed to the authorities, under pressure, that his accomplice was Scribes.

However, it was Hunt who was still racked with emotional virtue and responsibility. Not surprising to anyone; he was just that way.

Waiting at a stoplight, she adjusted her sunglasses. And her thoughts.

The crime seemed to be hanging over all their heads. And somewhere along the line, they would have to move on. The sentencing portion would take place in three months, but Elena was sure the first-time-offense teen would get off with probation and wouldn't sustain any risks. Scribes may not be so lucky.

Brent Dorsey's wife wasn't hurt from the incident, thank goodness. And Decker had plans to fix her windshield.

All in all, things could be a whole lot worse.

Yet the collateral damage had brought her need for patience to a whole new level.

Continuing through the green light, Elena took the opportunity to focus on Decker. She realized, for whatever reason, he had to experiment with the darker elements of life. She'd done it herself at that age, so her understanding stretched wide.

She looked in the rearview mirror and snickered. When she was thirteen, she'd gotten away with shoplifting a necklace she could've lived without.

Peer pressure was one mighty influence. She'd learned that a long time ago.

She arrived at the studio and unclenched her hands from the steering wheel, watching as her white knuckles returned to their normal color. Once inside the building, she observed all the professional photos on the white walls.

If only life could be this photogenic and pleasant.

She checked her watch: 10:03.

Where was the Klyce clan? Was this request so unreasonable?

Today she felt overly sensitive, unable to relax. Her instincts were on an all-time high.

Breathe in.

Hold.

Breathe out.

She had bartered with Yelden's when she produced a newspaper ad for a two-week special they were hosting, and they proposed that if she cut them a discount, they would offer her a free photo session.

After mentioning the special agreement to Hunt, he suggested, with careful consideration, they should all do a family portrait. Britni and Decker, as predicted, opposed the idea outright, but Hunt insisted that the notion would do all of them good. That it was time to start acting like a family. As a favor to him and Elena.

Upon registering with the person in charge, Elena found a seat in the lobby and filled in all the appropriate spaces of the information sheet.

She shivered. From the air-conditioning or from anger?

Why were they doing this to her? Even Hunt? Normally, he was Mr. Dependable.

Disrespect was one thing but inconsideration another. She and Pidge had been taught the total opposite, so that's why it bothered her.

She returned the paperwork. "The others should be here shortly," she informed the clerk through tight lips.

The peppy blonde looked past her to the empty waiting room. "Thank you, we'll be waiting."

Elena reseated herself and clasped her hands on her lap, fingers turning purple. She hoped her distress and forced smile didn't transmit on her face now, or in the picture.

She contemplated the photos she'd found in her mother's treasured albums up in the attic recently. By looking through them, at a different life, she'd been transported back to a child, on to a teenager, and finally to an adult. The progression from black-and-white images to color made her realize she'd had a constant sense of security that hadn't deviated from day one. But when the photographic timeline ended at the last page of the last album, she came to terms with being on her own. Her life in imagery with her parents was a blessed era only she could own.

Oh my, had things changed.

When today's pictures were developed, they would portray an existence so far removed from her family's that she no doubt wouldn't recognize the transformation.

The front door opened, bringing her back to the present. Those entering weren't there to meet her.

She consulted the wall clock: 10:13.

She called Hunt but he didn't pick up.

She must settle down, keep the tears from flowing, and figure in some endurance and faith that they would show. But from the media industry, she knew deadlines were crucial. The strategy had to be concise, even in the photo world.

This was just one more incident to extend her ongoing disappointment. She inhaled a concentrated breath, held it, then exhaled with a deep effort.

She found her compact within her purse and checked her appearance. Other than a stray eyelash on her cheek, all looked in place. Hairdo, well-coiffed. Makeup, nearly perfect. Salmon-colored top harmonizing the whole effect.

Good job, Elena!

The kids arrived a minute later. Britni and Decker that is, but no Hunt.

She got straight to the heart of the matter. "When I tell you ten o'clock, ten o'clock it is. Understood?" She forgot to censor her voice and her rebellious tone surprised even herself. *Where did that come from? Was it a command or a criticism?* "Where's your grandfather?"

The gap between permission and respect was still enormous. She wasn't a poster child of nastiness, but she had delved out her share of discipline.

They had all bridged a stalemate.

Was she becoming weaker? Or stronger?

Was she trying too hard? Or not hard enough?

"How the fuck would I know?" Decker shot back. "We haven't seen you guys in weeks." He said it less than enthusiastically as a look of vindication headed her way.

"Maybe he stopped in for a drink," Britni said, fluffing her hair. She glowed with some inner sense of glee.

Elena wasn't amused by her comment and Decker shot his sister a deliberate nonverbal insult.

Hunt's lateness was just a technicality. He'd be there very soon.

Right?

"Britni, please?" She failed to disguise her frustration. "Don't embarrass us." She felt like an apprentice who needed more lessons.

Elena suddenly took in Decker's slipshod wardrobe of ripped jeans and an untucked plaid shirt. It left plenty to be desired. Fighting an impulse to laugh, she reprimanded him again for his language. Her emotional state had a lot of company today as it was playing a game of hopscotch throughout her system. "Decker? Why?" She wasn't giving him any leeway even though she hadn't seen him for a while. In this case, absence hadn't made the heart fonder. "I've told you before, watch your mouth. I don't appreciate that kind of talk." The reiterated words were stern even by Elena's standards. "I know for a fact your mother, and your father, don't allow it either."

Had she not impressed upon the boy her displeasure every single instance?

Did her regulations mean anything?

As an adult in this footing, didn't she have the upper hand?

Her parents would never have allowed such language. And the sisters would never have spoken the words anyway, out of respect. Even if they had thought them.

101

She didn't make that many demands on this family. Why, oh why, couldn't they just accept the fact she wasn't going anywhere?

No matter how hard they tried to change that fact.

Even if she and Hunt weren't under the same roof, they would still have a relationship.

This kid could be infuriating one minute, and sweet the next. Like a song descending at the exact moment for effect. Or like a young lion not knowing when to pounce due to immaturity.

He slunk into a chair, head hunched between his shoulders. He was one incident away from adding to his already-grounded privileges or being kicked out of the house, but he didn't seem to care. "Yes, ma'am," he said with just enough attitude to make the point without saying any more. Dejection expressed itself in every line of his face.

Her sympathy only stretched so far.

Annoyance bubbled to the surface, but her lips remained clamped. Intuition received some bad moments while premonition was at full alarm. She just couldn't put her finger on the inner struggle's meaning.

It wasn't in her nature to be cruel, so why was she forced into being this critical? Maybe she was tired of being offended. However, someone had to take charge of these two. It was evident they were out to push her buttons.

"A certain amount of informality is permissible, but I've told you again and again, the word *fuck* is where I draw the line." Her whispered command was far from idle. A high state of temper cruised through her stamina at the same time the clerk interrupted the scene.

"We still have one more to show up," Elena told her.

"Okay, that's fine." The young girl glanced at the wall clock and walked away.

Elena kept up her integrity. She didn't take lightly to being shamed or disgraced, especially in public.

"Sorry," Decker offered with apparent irrelevance, giving in with a casual smile.

The apology was well deserved.

"That's better." She eased up on the scrutiny and discouraged the temptation to scream. She exhaled the breath she had been holding.

All the twists and turns were evident, and even intentional.

"Where's the mirror?" Britni piped in. "Do I look all right?" She underestimated her appearance. Today she looked remarkably tidy, carrying an abundance of decency, zeal, and a hint of expensive perfume.

"You look beautiful as always," Decker diagnosed with enough sarcasm to notice.

"Quit being rude," Britni snapped, ambling over to a jeweled wall mirror located in the hallway.

"Hey, you asked."

Elena felt as if she were between two fires with no way out and no clue which one to put out first.

But she'd be damned if she would let the kids know they were getting to her.

If only Hunt were here. They wouldn't act this way.

Taking a moment and glancing out the window, she questioned herself. Was she really gaining anything out of this relationship? How much longer could she remain impartial?

Was it truly time to part ways?

Resentment and skepticism jockeyed for position. For an instant, the attic plans trickled into her system and displayed hope.

She took in a deep breath and noticed the time.

10:20.

Suddenly, her phone beeped out its ring tone of a Beatles tune, and she saw Hunt's number on the screen.

"I'm on my way," he said when she answered. "You did say ten thirty, right?"

Is he serious? She couldn't believe it. Hadn't her fortitude experienced enough workouts for a while?

"No, Hunt, the appointment was for ten o'clock. We're all here waiting on you." Her tone climbed.

A brief silence was interrupted by a twenty-something man coming through the front door with a guitar case in tow. He was apparently there for his upcoming time slot.

"Oh, baby, I'm so sorry. I'm five minutes away," Hunt said.

"See you then." She clicked off the conversation with more-than-necessary emphasis, dismissing him without a goodbye. An instant headache pulsed.

Her mind tried to deny the situation, but how much more could she take?

Britni was slyly focusing on the lanky musician as he filled out his paperwork. She remembered being that age and having the same fascination with a similar physique. Elena blushed when the two made eye contact, both smiling.

Ah, memories.

Decker had slunk farther into the chair.

She gritted her teeth and tried to level her voice. "Decker, please sit up straight."

She didn't fit in this scene. Yes, they were going to take a picture and all, but the kids' careless manners were as noticeable as a restless lightning storm.

Would the conflict of interest show up in their faces in the portrait?

Would the wealth of pessimism shine through?

She had no idea what type of preventive measures to take against this dysfunctional family. She was glad the kids would be away from home for a few more weeks. Her conscience had been able to take a well-deserved sabbatical.

Until today.

"Fuck, we can't do anything," Decker murmured, straightening. "Is Granddad on his way? Dad's going to pick us back up at eleven." The last words were louder.

Elena rubbed her temples. "Can you please call him and ask him to make it a half hour later?"

He shrugged in reaction. "I suppose." He grabbed Britni's phone, as he was grounded from his, and made the call. With her preoccupation, his sister didn't even notice.

"Thank you."

She attempted to reason out the judgment she felt toward these kids. Neither were raised devout cowards. One of her hopes was that they weren't on drugs. But in this day and age, those clues could be well hidden.

While Decker talked with his dad, the clerk approached Elena again and asked if she would mind trading appointment times with the young man, who had a commitment and was on a time schedule.

"No, not at all." She waved her palms in the air. "Go right ahead." Always the negotiator.

The Klyce siblings gave her defensive stares.

How long would she remain in idle before the gears would be set in motion? Before all her sound rationale had been flushed out?

"Why'd you do that?" Decker stood up and glared at her. "Why can't we just go? Do this another time?"

Elena was in total agreement, but she couldn't respond adequately because her headache worsened.

Britni was oblivious to their conversation as she watched the curly-haired musician head down the hallway. A glint found its way into her eyes.

"We'll wait just a few more minutes. Your granddad's on his way."

Decker now paced in front of her.

Did she stand a chance against these kids and their established bond?

Her suggestion failed to materialize as an unforeseen paralysis gripped her. Under the strain and stress, she became dizzy. The air turned to paste as the chair became her enemy.

"Elena, you're as pale as a ghost," Britni shrieked. "What's wrong?"

"I dunno."

Both kids became a captive audience, listening with courtesy. A hug would have been more than welcome, but all the teenagers could do was gape. She felt similar to a popular exhibit at the state fair.

"Oh man! First Granddad doesn't show up, now this." Decker blinked as if from a knockout blow. He didn't appear ready for any responsibilities. "What next?"

So much for any sympathy. Their actions failed to give her any comfort.

Inhale.

Hold.

Exhale.

Peace.

Let go.

"Should I get some help?" Britni asked, lingering by Elena's side as she swayed to and fro.

A barrage of shadows, perhaps her own reflected twins, overcame Elena and she could not get an answer out of her dry mouth before she passed out in the chair.

Later on, she would swear she remembered Britni scream.

BEDTIME PRAYERS

Outside, the dirty, monotonous August rain had an attitude. Inside, the stillness of Elena and Hunt's bedroom was all-encompassing. They readied for bed, organizing their clothes and other items for work the following day.

The central air conditioning kept the space at a comfortable temperature, while the scent of Hunt's recent shower had nowhere to escape. He stood beside the bed, dressed only in pajama bottoms as he leafed through a mystery novel. "So," he broke the silence, "you want to tell me what's going on?" His question brimmed with aggravation.

"With what?" Across the room, Elena looked for her favorite turquoise pen in her large brown leather handbag, rifling through more stuff than she had anticipated. It wasn't in her nature to be this disorderly. Yet that's where she found herself these days.

In more ways than one.

"With everything." In the dim incandescent light of the nightstand lamps, his look and demeanor were four degrees short of quarrelsome. "I know how you think. How you operate." He threw the book on the bed.

She padded over and touched his arm with gentleness. "I'm going through a rough patch . . . something I can't explain. A midlife crisis, I suppose."

They sat side by side on the mattress.

"But, your fainting spell . . ." He narrowed his eyes and slipped an arm around her shoulder. "It worried the hell out of me." At the photographers', he'd walked in on the commotion as she was recovering. "And you wanna

106

just blow it off. Please, please go see your doctor." He softened the pleading by leaning into her.

"I will." She momentarily nestled her head into his neck.

Her blackout attacks, so far, hadn't affected her daily routine. She remembered having the same bouts during adolescence and attributed them to holding in her emotions. After all, her dad wouldn't let the girls have any kind of opinion or express their feelings. Not without repercussions. Was she experiencing the same side effect now?

"Promise?" He released his embrace and rubbed her back.

"Only if you do the same about *your* problem."

"What problem is that?" He issued a sideward glance.

Like you have to ask!

"Your drinking."

"Oh, God, not again." He let out an exasperated sigh and crossed his arms against his chest. "We get our lives halfway straightened out and you have to bring it up time after time. That's just wonderful."

Elena wasn't expecting the outburst; however, she knew she wasn't to blame.

She rose and faced him, her patience dissolved. "Excuse me? Don't you realize the reason I keep bringing it up is because it bothers me? Haven't I been through enough with all this?" She stopped mid-speech and squeezed her eyes shut.

A quiet and necessary interlude prevailed.

She made her way to her side of the bed. Their backs were to each other.

Is this what her parents went through? Her mother begging her father to ease up on the hard stuff?

"Are you *that* unhappy?" he asked. His tone was matter-of-fact.

She needed to heal her animosity or lose him. She wasn't quite ready for that.

Looking into the floor, she replied, "Oh, Hunt, I'm trying to figure it all out. Your drinking, the kids." She played with the knee of her silk pajama pants. "They can be such a handful. I want to be their friend, but they just won't let me." The longstanding issue cut a path of menacing anxiety through her mind. Somehow, she must put all involved on notice that things had to change. "I get so tired of the struggle."

He came around and knelt in front of her, caressing her forearms. His face brightened and a lock of his hair fell over his forehead. "Oh, baby, they promised me they'd have an attitude adjustment over the summer," he assured her. "But if they don't, I guess we'll just have to figure out something else."

She caressed the loose strand of his hair. Obligations were hard for Hunt. Hard in the sense that he had too many. Leaving his wife of twenty years to be with Elena had taken pure courage on his part, something he didn't have a great abundance of. Actually, the careless and irresponsible move had been out of character for him. It was one of those moments when one knew what he or she was made of.

Truth was, people closest to him had been shocked. After Gwen found out about the affair, she'd banished him from their home. He'd even got down on his knees to beg forgiveness, but she'd hear none of it. To her, his infidelity was a once-and-done type of milestone.

Which was fine—she'd done him and Elena a favor. Fate had brought them together, and they would maintain it. He'd fulfilled his obligation to his ex; she was out of his system. Even though, for months, his conscience had practically eaten him alive.

But now here the freed couple was at another crossroads.

And marriage wasn't a factor.

"I, more than anyone, want to get past this period." He rubbed the nape of his neck. "Find some kind of status quo."

She had allowed herself to sink so deep in thought that it was a shock when Hunt spoke.

"Status quo? How many times have I come after you at Paddy's because you were too drunk to drive?" Her anger proved essential.

It didn't help that she could smell remnants of whiskey.

Breathe deep.

During a lull in the conversation, the tension built. So did the tears in her eyes.

"And it seems like *you* always want to make waves." His intonation escalated, much like the rain outside. "Why do you always blame the kids for when things don't go right?"

Elena was sure he meant well, but the gentle growl came out too gruff. She had struck a nerve and had no response for him. Was that her goal? She hadn't intended to hurt him, but it was inevitable.

He stood up in a huff and left the room.

She massaged her left eyebrow and made her way to the closet to finalize tomorrow's outfit.

He returned immediately with a lowball glass of whiskey, raising a toast toward her.

She felt her shoulders tense. "Now *that* is making waves." Instinct told her to stop while she was ahead. "Goodnight," she declared, crawling into bed and turning off her light.

He eased down beside her, placing the drink on the nightstand, untouched.

"That is *my* way of coping," he murmured, the words coming out like an echo as his lower jaw sagged and he pointed to the glass.

"Can you please find another way? Not rely on liquor so much?" She switched the light back on. "For us?"

A clap of thunder startled both of them.

The delicate conversation resumed, affecting her more than she wanted. He was so handsome at that very moment she couldn't take her eyes off him.

"I'll try . . . I'll really try." He kissed her, giving her lips a much-needed endorsement.

"I'm sorry. Truly."

"Me too." A look of promise crossed his face.

She patted the dark stubble of his chin. Although she was comfortable within the confines of the covers, her mind raced with possibilities.

Would it be so bad to nurture this partnership for the long run?

She could do a whole lot worse in a partner.

At her age, she didn't want to get hurt again by anyone. The walls of protection were built quite solid. Would Hunt Klyce eventually betray her? Issue that heartbreaking license Gwen had received?

"I love you." He winked at her. The intensity in his eyes had cooled. "It's clear to me you've been talking to your sister again, haven't you?" His personal radar screen appeared to be up and running.

"Maybe." She swallowed hard, tightening the covers around her.

"I really don't like the idea of you going over there so often," he barked, dipping his chin. "What's wrong with talking to me?"

He didn't get it. Would never understand that there were way too many distractions under their roof for her to be able to focus, to pin him down.

"Don't blame Pidge. It's always me going to her." She was aware the comeback was more of a wail.

Had she scratched below the surface this time? Made him see that as long as she had Pidge, confiding in a man wasn't an option?

"Hon, has it ever occurred to you that you're trying to relive history by going to the Mortons? There's no returning to what used to be." The sullen words matched his scowl, penetrating her soul. "Things will never be the same again. As much as we'd all like them to be." He crawled over to his side of the mattress and found his way under the blankets.

She protested in silence, thinking about his words for a long moment. Was that what she was trying to do? Escape to the past where life was so much simpler?

"I realize that. I really do." She nodded and yawned. "But, it's my homestead. And as long as I can still have a part of it, I will." She fidgeted with a corner of the sheet. "How many people don't have that chance?"

He touched her gently on the cheek, yet his hand promised what he didn't give.

"I understand. *Yes*, the past was better. For me too." His eyebrows rose while he fidgeted with a pillow. "*Yes*, it was simpler. But what's important is *present day*." Hunt's perplexed speech was broken up in a chiding manner. "*Us*. Sometimes you scare me, as if the bygone days are more important than now, and the future." His expression transferred to sorrow.

He'd made his point. And he had every right to question her, to make her see the light. To call upon his senses to rein her in.

What exactly did she need to clear the way to fulfillment?

"It's not healthy, my love." He took her hand and played with her pinky finger. "Maybe you need to go see another psychologist."

She froze. That was Hunt's answer. Go see a professional. Leave it up to the counselors to set them straight once more. They had seen a specialist right after his divorce in hopes of starting fresh. The experience had been a positive strategy.

Now, however, she couldn't believe he was suggesting it. His statement contained just over six seconds' worth of words. But they devastated her completely. He'd pushed her past the gracious stage.

The day twenty-three years earlier when her own ex had admitted her into a mental rehabilitation facility because of a nervous breakdown was forever installed in her long-term memory. It remained a secret, even to Pidge. The short overnight stay was the most profound chapter of her life, the turning point to rise up and find strength.

Whatever it took, she'd fight her way against the likelihood of ever being in a place like that again. At the time, she'd had nowhere to go but forward.

Right now, the feeling proved similar.

"Or, could be, you just need something . . ." He permitted cleverness to edge his mindset. ". . . different." He sat up straighter. "Like a hiatus? A vacation?" He positioned his torso on one elbow. "Would you like that? We could go somewhere in a couple of weeks," he added quickly, encouraging forgiveness, never one to hold a grudge. "When the Nalplex project is done

Yes, I'd like that. A cruise like Pidge had mentioned sounds wonderful!

By myself, thank you very much.

I need downtime, a break, away from you, away from your grandchildren. I've been punished enough.

Maybe I'm just surrounded by too many Klyces.

"I don't know. I think I simply need my energies rechanneled, but I don't know how," she said with a wry grin. "It's like I'm trapped by my decisions, right or wrong." Even though she'd doubled up on her meditation time, she could still use some kind of boost.

A cool blast of air from the overhead vent seemed to bring the mood back to near-normal.

"My poor baby." He ran his knuckle over her nose. "I'll never let you go. I love you." His eyes danced with obedience. "I may not be husband material, but I'm devoted to you," he said, an intense look deeded upon his square face.

They hadn't mentioned marriage for the past year. When they were first together, that was all they talked about. He had claimed his undying loyalty. Now that they were settled into a comfortable routine, matrimony was rarely discussed. Like a verbal contract had been broken.

Guess there were undue distractions getting in the way.

111

However, she was curious if she would accept a serious proposal.

"Besides, we belong together. We're too good together." It sounded like an afterthought; the words seemed shallow.

Every so often, she had to wonder if he talked via liquor or his heart. She'd like to think it was the latter, but she couldn't tell anymore. He swore he had eased up on the booze, but Hunt was a drinker who could fool a minister if need be.

Was she truly ready to move on? Maybe she was just destined to be alone, simple as that.

If she were to make a move in that direction, would time still be on her side? Would she find the happiness she longed for elsewhere?

Granted, their sex was the greatest she had ever known. As of late, she considered their passion similar to a cinder fire. It could be left to smolder or raked to spark the flames again. Presently, it festered.

But was the intimacy enough? Why wasn't she content?

Why couldn't one decision override the other so both could get on with their lives? Her psyche had taken enough of a beating.

"Let's not argue the point," he said. Another round of kissing pardoned the previous conversation. "Go to sleep and we'll talk about it later." By the way he said it, she could tell he was in the before-sleep stage. "Okay?"

"Agreed," she said with sharp relief.

"Okay. If it's all the same to you, I need sleep. I'm beat. I have a full day ahead of me with meetings and proposals. What's more, a good night's sleep will clear the air," he explained, switching off the bedside light. "I love you."

"Ditto," she said drowsily, disinclined to undertake any more disputes tonight.

Within minutes, a round of his feeble snoring followed.

The tears Elena had blinked away earlier overflowed and wet her cheeks. She closed her eyes and changed the direction of her thoughts.

She saw in her mind's eye the bedroom of her youth, all those long years ago.

The room had been a study in pink. The bed's chenille spread cradled a storybook doll smack in the middle of the fluffy pillows. Throughout the space were toys like paper dolls, animal rummy cards, games of Cootie and Monopoly, jacks, stuffed animals, a viewmaster.

Those were the days of riding bikes without helmets, playing with schoolmates all day long on Saturday. Days when there were no worries about weight, major risks, and Dad or Mom solved her immediate problems.

After she turned old enough, the bookshelves became lined with the Trixie Belden, Donna Parker, and Annette series of books. In time, posters of the newest rock group plastered the walls.

No matter her age, she would always remember her youth as being secure, safe. Her parents were in the next room in case of storms, nightmares, or sicknesses. Oh, if only her mother were here to tuck her in these days, to tell her everything was going to be fine.

Those happy times of family union were gone. Through college, marriages, careers, and romances, she'd never recaptured a parallel of the Vaughn Springs years. Regardless of who was in the picture or how old she was.

Drying her tears on the sheet, she contemplated the present.

Was Hunt Klyce guaranteed to stick around? To provide for her when it was absolutely necessary?

The others had promised, too, but the circumstances served as downfalls.

Or had her stern midlife independence diminished the desire to buckle down with the man beside her? Sure, he had his own set of problems, but in the end, was it *she* who wasn't satisfied? And kept finding excuse after excuse to jeopardize their relationship?

Even if she were to leave, he would come after her and they would reconcile. She was certain of it. Because he was the kind of man who wouldn't be able to stand her with anyone else.

In the end, she should be grateful he cared that much for her.

A faint flash of lightning illuminated the room, alerting her that it was time to close out the evening.

In the old days, she would say a nighttime prayer, thanking the Lord for her family, her friends, a good day. What did the kids today pray for? No more terrorism or mass shootings? No more wars? To wake up? Or did they even pray?

The scare factors back then were unbelievable, almost nonexistent. The only things she had been frightened of were the dark, the bogeyman, and God. It was a totally different world now.

At present, did Elena Polson have anything left to pray for? Her partner and her sister were right: there was no going back. It stood to reason there was no restoring times past.

At least she had enjoyed them, had experienced them. Had lived them to the best of her abilities.

Her deliberation ran out of steam, and she, too, dozed off. As she slept into the wee hours, she concentrated on those dreams she had left.

I'LL STAND BY YOU

Hunt awoke just as Elena fell asleep, the appalling stillness of the house unsettling him because he had become used to most of the rooms being constantly lived in.

This was a hell of a time for his mind to wander. The work site budget was due three days ago, and tomorrow he needed to concentrate and draft his proposal to finish the project. The undertaking demanded everything he had to give. And he'd ignored the deadline long enough.

Tonight's events didn't help the cause.

He'd never understand why his drinking bothered Elena so. It wasn't that he misbehaved or abused her, or anyone. He was aware that her father drank to excess, so perhaps that component was to blame for her defensive temperament on the matter.

Staring at the dark ceiling, he placed his crossed hands behind his head. He realized there was no way he could ask her to move out. With her fainting spells and the possible transfer of her business to Vaughn Springs, the strain would be too much. Coupled with Decker's small-time crime, he himself couldn't take any more bombshells. He'd have to let it play out. And hope they'd all find that peace he knew was on the horizon.

The thought warmed his soul.

In the dim light, he peeked over at his partner, now asleep on her back. Her hair was gathered in a ponytail atop her head, and she had the bedcovers bundled up at her neck. A peaceful, childlike look resided on her face, complete with a faint smile. He could still detect the moisturizing cream she had used on her skin. As much as he wanted to touch her cheek, he refrained.

Oh, how he loved her. That fact couldn't be denied.

At their best, they made such a great team together, despite all the differences.

Their relationship was a stark contrast to his with Gwen. He hated comparing the two, but his ex-wife had been dull, unkind, and fussy in her nature, while Elena was compassionate, sensitive, and witty. Yet her reserved manner always gave him plenty of anxiety. He still had to guess at some of her actions and reactions.

He rolled over and settled his body within the covers. He reflected on the scene before this evening's major confrontation. She had eagerly told him of the attic plans. How she would give up her downtown office and redecorate the room at the Mortons, and what it would mean to her creativity to be back in her element. She was beyond thrilled as her ideas had unfolded.

He hadn't seen her that happy in ages.

"That sounds wonderful," he had reluctantly encouraged her, not one to begrudge her exhilaration. "If you think that's what you really want."

"I do." Her reply had been swift.

"Well, you know best." He'd spoken humbly. In all honesty, he had her best interests at heart.

As he mulled it over now, he realized the time and setting had been perfect to address his own suggestion that she temporarily move out when the kids returned after the summer. Try to convince her he'd be doing her a favor.

All things considered, would it be the right thing? Or just another defeat to add to his resumé?

Integrity was so important to him. After the split with Gwen, his mission seemed bona fide. It had been almost all-consuming at the time because the guilt had just about eaten him alive. So far, he believed himself capable of dealing with any situation that might arise.

Like the report lingering on his desk at work.

Geez! Buckle down, mister!

He inhaled with all his might. When the kids got back in a few days, Britni would be in her last year of high school and Hunt would make every effort to steer Decker in the right direction, more than a push or shove. He might possibly get the boy a part-time job after school and weekends to give him some responsibility.

One with no distractions.

Steepling his fingers in the dark, he prayed that Jony's cure was only weeks away and that by then, she would be well enough to handle her own children. The plan would delight him to no end. Then, it would be his and Elena's turn again for quality time; their moment to settle down and get back on track.

Could she wait it out?

Could they recover the magic?

He secretly longed to marry her, but he had to be cautious after ending his twenty-five-year marriage. Plus, the timing must be right to propose. After all, he still believed in destiny and didn't want to give up on another relationship. Although, coupled with Elena's insecurity, he realized he risked losing her to better prospects.

Optimism chased doubt around his brain. Being back in Vaughn Springs might make Elena consider living there with Pidge and Bill instead of facing any more problems with him. Turn the attic into a writing studio *and* studio apartment. She might have even already contemplated along these same lines.

He rubbed his eyes. He wouldn't blame her if she chose not to stick around and endure any more provocations. He knew she could be self-supporting—her history proved that reality. Except for the time the Mortons had taken her in after her last failed relationship. The circumstances were such back then that she didn't have a choice.

More thoughts kept him from sleep as he noticed the clock inching toward midnight. He had yet to figure out why being in her hometown was so important to Elena. Was there something she wasn't telling him? Wasn't it taking steps backward instead of forward? That part bothered him the most. She had the tendency to glorify the past as if it was still part of her existence. Ever the visionary, he wanted the present and future realms of her life, so how was he to cope with her mindset? He didn't have any easy answer.

Further, the fact that she consulted her sister time and again troubled him, too. He could never compete with that union, and frankly, he didn't want to. He had been just as close to his two brothers until their parents' death and the estate settlement put them at odds. The siblings seldom spoke to one another now. Even though they all lived in the same town.

He caressed his goatee, debating with himself what it would mean if Elena did indeed move out. She'd made a great go-between in challenging times, together with the fact he enjoyed having an equal partner. In the end, he delighted in snuggling up to a warm body, especially hers. She had a certain power that attracted all his senses. During sex, she always made him feel like a teenager.

Even at his age.

Thinking ahead to if she did leave, he'd probably still go to bed at ten o'clock each night, occasionally have his recurring dream of being washed ashore from a boating accident, and wake up to the alarm at six every morning, followed by a silent prayer for seeing another day. Then he'd work a ten-hour day five or six times a week, depending on the weather. If the kids were still under his roof, he wouldn't be able to stop in at Paddy's Wagon and partake in a drink or two every night, a routine it had taken him years to build.

At the moment, he heard his partner's deep-sleep purrs. Goodness, how he would miss her if she were to leave. His inclination was that he'd be lonely beyond belief. However, when it came down to it, the kids were his priority: they needed his guidance and love. He wouldn't deny them that. They depended on his sacrifice and loyalty whether they realized it or not.

He just wished Elena was in on the plan.

But he understood if she didn't want to be.

With that notion, he squinted at the clock. Eighteen past midnight. Good heavens! He turned on the CD player for the customary and relaxing sleep music. Elena had introduced him to the steady ritual two years ago. With or without her, he'd continue that habit also.

He shifted to his other side and hauled the bedcovers up to his shoulders. By 12:20 a.m., he was snoozing to the sounds of a cello contending with ocean waves.

AS IT SHOULD BE

Back at work on a hot September day, Elena checked her emails before delving into a print ad for the local newspaper. The air conditioning tempered the interior of the renovated building to coolness in contrast to the dazzling heat reflected from the asphalt outside.

She noticed nothing alarming in her contacts, so she switched on her LED desk lamp and began her task.

The client was Robel's Furniture Store, who had utilized her services before. The angle she wanted to feature this time was that the quality of Robel's valuable pieces is unmatched and can take the shifting and handling undergone when someone moves houses.

The graphics in the ad would show a transport van and the movers would have bubble memes declaring to the owners: "Oh, you have furniture from Robel's! No problem! We'll handle it with special care!" Another option would be: "Bob, we have another load from Robel's Furniture." And Bob would reply: "Thank heavens! It always makes the job easier."

A whiff of strong coffee crept under the door from the cooperative office across the hallway from her, interrupting her train of thought. She didn't drink java herself, but the aroma had become a staple during her working hours. Would she miss this all someday?

The windowless ten-by-ten brick room she rented contained one bookshelf holding old magazines for inspiration and her vintage Philco desktop radio, a good luck charm of sorts. Over her corner desk, two motivating seascape portraits hung, while an acrylic award she had won for a bank's ad campaign sat on her uncluttered desk.

There was little space for much else besides the office chair and printer stand. The building itself was a renovated former opera house that would never be free of its glorious theatrical atmosphere. Her area had been used as a dressing room. Many times, Elena imagined what it must have been like one hundred years ago. Women in their sober-colored gowns and men donning Edwardian fashion, waiting to go on stage.

Often, the thoughts aided her inspiration.

She took a sip of her bottled water and snacked on carrot and celery sticks, surveying the unfinished material before her.

Reflections of relocating her *own* furnishings to Pidge's attic came to mind and proved significant. She consoled herself with ideas of how she would center her desk in front of the lone window, brighten up the room with white paint, hire electricians to wire for more outlets and internet access, construct an outside stairway and entry door, and change all her correspondence to the new address—basically start over. There would be lots to do.

The transformation would do her good and she couldn't wait for the challenge. That room always uplifted her, and she yearned for the tranquility on a daily basis.

At least in the career realm of her life. Personally, not much had changed since the grandkids had returned three weeks ago.

So much for the promise of attitude adjustments.

A loud crash outside her door raised her pulse a few notches.

"Sorry, folks!" yelled the artist two doors down. "Clumsy me! Everything's okay!"

Elena snickered and shook her head, calming down.

She had to wonder, in the end, if she would be more productive and successful in a remote quiet room. Would she find the new studio her safe working haven?

Or would it serve as a place to hide away, like it always had been for her?

Yes, the attic was her go-to refuge, somewhere she could be totally alone and figure out life. Time and time again.

However, the business of freelance copywriting had its benefits. She loved the facets of no one to answer to, setting her own deadline and working at her own pace, all the opportunities she found online, the networking process, and the right amount of stress. As a marketing tool, she had recently launched an e-newsletter to engage her contacts on her freelance business status and services. Just to keep her name out there in the community.

Yet there were times she spent spinning her wheels and enduring hours upon hours of loneliness.

Those were the downsides of this entrepreneurship.

Having steady work, as before, granted more freedom and benefits not otherwise afforded with one's self-employment. But she'd made her choice and was happy with her professional vocation.

Every now and then, she got together with former colleagues and a handful of hometown friends, ones she'd had for decades. They gave her the social balance for interpersonal relationships a man or work couldn't provide. She cherished those quality times.

When she made the move to Vaughn Springs, she hoped she would still be able to count on the help of the graphics student in the present adjoining chamber. Josh had been a tremendous asset to her ad campaigns—so tech-savvy and creative. If he couldn't carry on, she didn't know what she'd do. She'd just have to cross that juncture if it came.

Today, she had brought the flute along. For a momentary mental break, she picked it up and began a tune from memory. Then another, and another. Short bursts, but helpful. She was sure the other tenants could hear her, but she didn't care. The instrument had become her best friend, taking her mind off her troubles.

Soon, she was playing a favorite piece from her college days. It was incredible how after all these years she could remember it.

Talk about stimulation!

She turned on the radio to her favorite classic rock station and played along with the harmony of a bygone song. Elated, she allowed her fingers the ease of artistry, the notes floating upward as if she were in an open-air pavilion. An expert she was not, but deep inside, she'd discovered one of the answers her soul had been searching for.

How could she have let this talent slide all these years?

The passion of the flute had revived her. She was ready to tackle the final elements of the ad.

As with every completion, she asked herself a series of questions: Would newspaper readers take action from the ad and find reason to visit said advertiser? Could she persuade customers to shop at the targeted business? How would prospects benefit from the copy? In turn, would the effort even be appreciated by the client? Does it all really matter?

If most answers were positive, she'd carried through her job.

Yes, she found copywriting rewarding. If luck prevailed, she'd be at this for years to come.

She still had her dreams of a website presence, of getting her name out there. The world was changing and she knew she'd have to change with it. A tough component of the venture included knowing and understanding a particular audience relating to the product or service. Important factors took skill and research. She had to figure out what customers wanted and weren't receiving, in addition to focusing their problems and helping them achieve their goals. A copywriter must take prospective consumers on a narrative journey, and make it all believable.

With her attention completely absorbed, she managed to accomplish a bewildering amount of detail in a short span of time. If only she could formulate that same strategy at home.

She stood up and pump-fisted into the air.

Satisfied with the ad, she made the appropriate call to her contact at Robel's Furniture. While she waited for his voicemail to pick up, the line beeped to signal an incoming call. She connected to it.

"Is this Elena Polson?" inquired an unrecognizable female voice on the other end.

"Yes." Curiosity blended with intuition.

"This is Nurse Hammond calling from Worden General Hospital."

The words confirmed Elena's anguish. "Okay."

"We admitted a Hunt Klyce today and he's asking for you." The speech was all right, but the tone was all wrong.

"What?" Panic tore through her. "How? Why?"

"I'm sorry, I can't divulge any more details." She paused. "I'm just relaying the information."

Elena's hand shook so hard the phone dropped onto her lap.

So much for a good day.

The fleeting delusion proved about as genuine as her vulnerability.

Inhale.
Hold.
Exhale.
Patience.

ONE MORE FOR THE ROAD

Elena put on her best face as the physician passed on enough information to fill in most of the minor details of Hunt's condition. The report confirmed her suspicions.

Drunk driving.

He'd been involved in a one-car accident just blocks from home, hitting a utility pole.

"Your husband's in serious condition," Doctor Cavallo diplomatically clued her in, his speech cold and deliberate.

The tough delivery penetrated.

She held on to her response, especially the one to apprise him they weren't married. She could only nod her tilted head in understanding. Because the room didn't pass the smell test, nausea coursed through her. Joined with a weakness, she felt like she had just finished a harrowing roller coaster ride.

Was it Hunt's dilemma? Or something else? Her jangled nerves handled the news, but in the flesh, something else was going on. She didn't recognize her own symptoms and her concern took on relevance.

"He'll need rest, foremost." The physician's crisp voice was roughened by a faint accent.

"All right." The words broke.

Hunt's hospital room seemed as cold and still as a playground in stark winter. Eerily quiet, as if it held a long breath. The only sounds came from the beeps of the equipment and Hunt's smooth snoring.

To her, it was a scene suitable for those unfamiliar with these kinds of circumstances. Like herself.

She peered down at her partner. His tanned features were loose, with an unconscious false smile that refused to fade, as if he had been deported to a paradise with no worries to be had. His slim, handsome fingers—ones that had brought her many an orgasm—rested motionless on his chest. This was all like looking through a camera lens by way of a wrong angle.

Oh, Hunt, what have you done?

With all the recent events, he needed this break. But what a way to get it.

When drunk, Hunt Klyce was no harm to anyone but himself. A quiet lush. But tonight, he was in the hospital. She wondered how much he had drank.

Add to that, she had no idea what condition his truck was in, or if he would be charged with some kind of offense. For that matter, would Paddy's Wagon be involved? Her next step would be to contact the police.

"Oh, babe, why couldn't things be different?" The statement hitchhiked through her mind and graced her thoughts. "Why, oh why, do you have to drink? . . ."

As she explored the state of affairs in her mind, she wondered how long she could excuse away his faults. How long could she feed her uneasy consciousness and live with an element of suspense?

She settled into the bedside chair, recalling the time Hunt had left a healthy bonfire burning in a huge wind. And he was nowhere to be found. The flames had come within inches of the house when, by chance, the wind had died down and the fire followed suit.

Common sense that day had been in short supply.

And those occasions he'd called her from the bar wanting a ride home weren't far from her reflections either. At least he had contacted her and not taken up with a stranger, which could have ended in more dire consequences.

She shut her eyes for a minute.

Paddy's Wagon.

His favorite hangout, the local drinking establishment he'd taken her to on more than one occasion when they were dating. The place was innocent enough. For the most part, everyone there knew each other. Perhaps that was part of the attraction; he was comfortable among a group of like-minded people.

She'd tried hard to not be a hypocrite because she'd filled a few glasses of wine herself, especially when trying to be sociable with him. But enough was enough. She and he had been derailed in far too many instances. She was ready to move on to the next phase—if indeed there was one for them.

Life after Paddy's Wagon.

Even liquor can't hold back tomorrow.

She flung open her eyes when a petite blonde nurse entered. They greeted each other, then the caretaker switched on the overhead light, checked Hunt's readings, and quickly departed.

But soon afterward, Elena discovered her mind refused to keep off the subject of the whole dilemma. Even her nausea needed focus. Both incidences were playing an overture in her system.

Was it the odor of the hospital? Or the emotional trauma peddling around her mind?

Categorically speaking, her post-menopausal status still kept a vigil. Even after eight years, it very well could be the cause.

The knuckles of her hands strained white as she clenched the arms of the chair. Frustration bridged disappointment and soon must strike a balance into buoyancy.

The fear of losing this man before her undermined her sensibility.

Many of Hunt Klyce's emotions were as deep and open as some of the gorges of the Grand Canyon. Mainly those concerning regret and pleasure. He was the kind of person who'd rather risk his life than ruin it.

Keeping her gaze glued to him, she remembered the occurrence early in their relationship when she had discovered him in the bathroom crying his eyes out in a drunken state, going on and on about how he had left his wife. The guilt had practically engulfed him.

To this day, she couldn't be one hundred percent certain that if Gwen wanted him back, he wouldn't go.

She leaned forward and took one of his warm hands through the bedrails. The rest of his body was wrapped in standard white hospital covers. His usual straight posture looked slumped and defeated.

Upon further reflection, she recalled a point in time when one of his drinking buddies had cozied up to her and Hunt was oblivious to the action.

126

His attention had been turned to the football game on the television set in the adjacent room. He hadn't even noticed Elena and Joel in the kitchen, amicably talking it up.

Joel's legendary cowboy looks had worked on her vulnerability while his shady azure-blue eyes always seemed to give her the impression he was ironically putting her body under a microscope for dissection. She didn't mind the attention.

Back then, she wasn't getting much of it from Hunt.

Up to this day, in her mind, the man remained as one of her back-burner candidates. She didn't have the slightest desire to repeat the indiscretion, but if she felt inclined to even the score, she would.

Just in case Hunt did to her what he did to Gwen.

She'd live with the emotional consequences afterward. Crazy as it sounded.

Hunt twitched in his sleep and startled her, and with it came a sudden application of cold logic.

She rose and stood over him, caressing a lock of stick-straight hair back into place above his forehead. She'd much rather be elsewhere, ruffling his healthy head of hair the way she had in their more playful periods.

"All this is going to work out for the best, my love," Elena said with determination, wondering if he would be able to hear her. "Whatever comes our way." The statement disappeared from her lips.

She took in a deep breath, making her way to the window. Thankfully, her queasiness had subsided.

Darkness had descended outside and she realized she must call the kids. They had to be wondering where they were. She found her phone and dialed Britni. As best she could, she explained the situation. The girl surprised her by seeming reasonably pleased Elena had let her and Decker know the news.

The sudden change-up in Britni's attitude delighted her, making the imminent defensive irritation vanish. It was a relief because she had steeled herself long ago for unsuitable responses.

On the whole, she'd grown accustomed to sarcasm.

With a sigh of relief, she had to ask herself if she was being unreasonable with her feelings. Why did she always have to assume the worse?

Had Hunt and the kids brought her to the point of no return before she shut down?

After this latest development, was she up to any more challenges with his drinking binges? Or, for that matter, with his grandchildren's shenanigans?

She was tired, so very tired, of carrying the entire emotional load.

She didn't care to fight the uncertainties any longer. She was getting too old. The realization may be slow going, but it was valid nonetheless.

If only I could want nothing more than what I have at the moment, Elena considered, almost as a reflex. *It would make all the difference in the world.*

Yet she was no closer to a solution than when this dilemma started.

Meanwhile, Elena was going to put Hunt on notice: the alcohol or her. Period.

Compromise was out of the question. A refocus would set things straight. Neither one of them could allow for any more mistakes.

She stretched her arms above her head and rotated her neck.

This wasn't exactly the worst of times, but it seemed mighty close. Between Hunt's accident, Decker's crime, Britni's cynicism, and the possibility of moving her office, this dysfunctional life had taken on the feeling of permanence.

Oh, how she could use a meditation session!

"Babe." The word dangled in midair before she discovered it came from Hunt. He then reacted with a shudder and a look of fear. "What the—" With a sharp intake of breath, he tried rising up in bed, but straightaway was resisted by fatigue.

"It's okay, hon. You're in the hospital." Even in her ears, the confession sounded raw, incomplete. She tried to smile, but failed. She clasped a hand over his; it felt waxy, like a cornstalk.

Apprehension began preying again.

His eyes answered the unspoken question. Yes, he had been drunk. And the alcohol was probably still in his system.

She allowed a silence. The bitter taste in her mouth reminded her of a cheap wine she'd had in the past. How ironic.

"Did I lose much blood?" he moaned, gingerly glancing around for bearings. A change came over the handsome features of his face. She thought the illumination from the light over the bed sharpened the angle of his jaw and pointed up his cheekbones.

128

Concern emerged once more. "What are you talking about?" she asked.

"When the guy"—his labored words shocked the air—"shot me."

"What? What guy?" she gasped. "Shot?" She stared at him intently. Had she missed something?

"The gun . . . I . . ." His expression, and voice, were as cold as the Arctic pole and about as remote. His eyes and lips shut and the room became silent again.

She could think of nothing else to say.

She turned to find relief and the doctor entered, alarming her and interrupting her reverie.

"Doctor, you didn't tell me the whole story. He was shot!" she whispered loudly, feeling as if she were witnessing this situation instead of being a participant.

"Excuse me? Oh, no, no . . . he had to have been dreaming that." The dismay in his face was a sufficient answer. "Sometimes, under these circumstances, recollections become inconsistent," he conceded, reassuring her as he rubbed his hands together. "With the medication, he's probably hallucinating." He stood over the bed.

The explanation was as vague as a campaign promise.

"Oh." The pitch of Elena's tone decreased a notch while her chest pressure lightened.

Hunt's breathing became normal again as he appeared to return to dreamland.

"You know, we see a lot of cases like this," the doctor said, staying on point while he jotted down a few notes on his electronic tablet. "And we conclude that it's not *why* the patient drinks, but because of *whom*."

The steady, thin flow of the accusation hit her like a slap across the face as he took her elbow and guided her away from Hunt.

For a moment, she couldn't speak. "I understand." She folded her arms at chest level. "That's a pretty powerful statement." She hesitated. "But one to be explored." Had her mother received a similar allegation during her parents' worst days?

"I'm sorry." He looked down into the floor. "We just see a lot of these cases."

"However"—she narrowed her eyes and jutted her chin—"I *do* object to being criticized." She was satisfied with herself for speaking up.

"I'm not laying the blame on anyone in particular as I'm not familiar with the circumstances." He scratched his neck. "It was just a general observation. Again, I apologize."

"Thank you. And thank you for all you're doing. Any idea when I can take him home?"

"That remains to be seen," he said with resignation. "Let's see what today brings." With that, he shuffled out the room.

She had to remain optimistic that the prognosis would be positive.

In the wake of all the turmoil, she knew she needed a break. Dodging all the equipment in the room and making her way into the hallway, she hastened her steps toward the main exit. Outside, she found comfort in fresh air and a sweeping lawn.

Beyond that, the first hint of a September dawn infused the skyline. Was it really the next day? There was not an ounce of wind. She took a seat on a bench as a cool dampness triggered through her.

As she fretted, she knew she had to sort out the solutions to this latest quandary. The last twelve hours had felt like she was stuck in a revolving door with no way out.

More thoughts made their presence known. To her, they were like peering at a roadmap to nowhere.

Was this all too big for her? She couldn't afford any more mishaps or accidents. No more shocking news or gloom.

This was it.

Even her meditation couldn't center her anymore.

She had a business to run, and a looming deadline she had to meet later on today. Too much was at stake. She must find the energy and innovation to create an unforgettable ad for a new jewelry business in town. Forthwith, it received priority.

If only Hunt would come up behind her, tap her on the shoulder and say, "Let's go home and forget this and start over."

Now *she* was dreaming.

The streets picked up more traffic while the sky took on added color, looking larger than the earth, as if there might be enough to tuck in around the edges. Another day of imminent changes on the horizon.

On this date, Elena Polson would find strength and decide she would carry this thing with Hunt through to the finish. Because right now starts forever. How ever long that may be.

She had to stay true to her original purpose of finding security and peace in her life, and someone to share it with. She couldn't lose sight of the objective.

She loved the man inside this hospital. Loved him like no other. She'd discovered that just an hour ago.

And she was sure he'd agree to her truce and hold court on any middle ground at stake.

Take a breath.
Hold.
Blow it out.
Peace.

SOMEWHERE IN-BETWEEN

Home from the hospital one week later, Hunt sat in his recliner and rotated his left ankle. It had been sprained in the accident. Elena sat beside him on the couch as they watched a rerun of a popular sit-com. She looked over at him and muted the sound.

"Still hurt as bad?" she asked.

"Yeah, I can't believe it didn't break." His forehead puckered. "Thank goodness for pain pills."

They discussed his impending OVI charge—operating a vehicle under the influence of alcohol—and subsequent reimbursement to the Worden Municipal Utility Company for the pole he'd damaged. On top of all that, his four-year-old truck needed repair.

Although he didn't remember taking a blood-alcohol-content test at the scene, luckily he had, because with Ohio laws, he otherwise could have had his driver's license suspended. That would have changed the landscape of their daily routine.

"Bet you're happy with all this." He looked at her with a fixed stare.

She could use one of his winks, but he didn't oblige.

"Why's that?" She bit her bottom lip. "How could I possibly be pleased with you facing potential jail time?" She paused, squinting her eyes. "Not to mention the cost of all the fines?"

In a strange way, all this had worked in her favor. Now he would be forced to quit drinking and stopping at Paddy's Wagon. However, he could potentially bump up his consumption at home.

Not an option she wished to consider.

"Oh, baby, forgive me." He reached for her hand. "I'm so sorry."

She felt his warmth through his touch. But the action seemed inappropriate. "At least you weren't hurt any more than you were. And no one else was involved."

"True. Now we need to be concentrating on your health, on what's going on with you." He slipped his hand away and reached for the glass of soda by his side. "Before something else comes up. In this family, any number of things could happen." A snicker dangled at the corner of his lip.

She had Googled her medical symptoms and didn't discover any alarming information, but she thought it best to see her doctor for a checkup. It had been a few years since she'd gone and the urgency held authenticity.

Plus, Hunt was right. In the throes of another school year, further sets of problems could crop up at any time with this bunch. Their history had proved it over and over again.

Momentarily, Britni joined them. A heavy shampoo scent followed her. An odd look, furtive and secret, slipped over her unadorned face, almost like a mask. Even devoid of makeup, she was radiant. "I need to tell you both something." Her words weren't without charm as she stood before them, rubbing her throat.

Elena turned off the television with the remote and studied the girl's firm chin. There was an unfamiliar slump in her shoulders. She'd never seen her so serious. Her normally ambitious nature was on hiatus.

A long shaft of early-October fading sunshine struck through the space between the television screen and Britni, dust motes dancing a lively rumba in the light.

But deep down, Elena knew the answer without the question. Even without being a mother, her intuition springboarded into action.

"Please don't judge me. I don't need that right now." Anxiety and mystery intermingled in an equal blend in the girl's request. "But . . ." She closed her liquid-blue eyes and drew in a deep breath. "I'm pregnant." Her voice fell and she eased down beside Elena.

Bewildered, Elena's eyes and mouth opened to their full extent, but no words emerged. She felt similar to a tourist in a foreign land: not in the know. She observed, with pity, Britni's trembling hands. And also how the room's ambience heightened the surprising red glint in her dark hair. She intercepted a glance from Hunt. A flush had spread across his face, and his fingers rested against his mouth. He, too, was speechless.

The silence must have confused and alarmed the teen. She opened her eyes and her gaze roamed around the room.

"Are you sure?" Elena asked. The seat on the couch had suddenly become uncomfortable. "How can you be so certain?"

"I took three over-the-counter tests, and they all came back positive." Elena could see that tears were within striking distance, yet Britni kept up her genuine rhetoric.

It had taken guts to approach her elders and confess this revelation, given the fact they'd granted her an independence they had both lacked in their own adolescence.

"How far along are you?" Elena asked with as much concern as she could muster. She was clueless how this worked, the next steps that needed to be taken.

And from all appearances, Hunt was indignant. Stiff as a soldier at attention, he still hadn't responded.

"As far as I can tell, I'm four months."

Elena and Hunt shook their heads almost simultaneously.

Elena assumed the lead, rubbing her thumb's knuckle. "Okay, so, what is your plan? Where is the father? For that matter, who is he?" She fumbled in her deliverance, attempting not to scrutinize. She realized her own hands shook.

At this point, maybe she should ask easier questions.

Even with all the other teenagers' drama, how could she have overlooked such a major change in Britni? For God's sake, she was four months pregnant. Why had the girl chosen now to disclose the shocking development, knowing Hunt just had an accident? What an illogical call.

She'd never understand the rationale behind these kids' objectives. Were they that disconnected from reality?

"It happened over the summer. When I was at Dad's." Britni sniffed, managing a deadpan expression. "It was a heat-of-the-moment thing. A summer fling, as you people would call it." The sarcasm worked this time. "The guy's not even on my radar."

Hunt still had no input. He folded his arms across his chest and stared at his bandaged ankle.

"Oh my God," Elena interjected in a near whisper. She cocked her head and shook it.

As they listened to Britni's earnest, energetic voice dole out what details she dared share, an aura of sympathetic credence surrounded her.

Elena's mind drifted. The girl was too young to be a mother, had too many dreams yet ahead of her, especially college. If only she would have slowed down the rush and pressure of that crucial moment. Judgment would have had a better chance to take hold and guide her away from wrong behavior.

But it was too late. With Britni's four-month pregnancy, she wouldn't be able to hide the obvious in another month.

On impulse, Elena scooted over and hugged her. The rosemary scent of shampoo filled her nostrils. "We'll figure it out, sweetie," she pledged gently. "We're in your village now." She pursed her lips.

Britni accepted the embrace. She wouldn't have weeks ago.

"Right?" Elena's low-pitched word was directed toward Hunt.

"Indeed," he said at last.

"And . . . I want to have the child," Britni announced positively. "It's not a matter for discussion." Fortitude caught in her voice as she peered at each of them. Her flawless face almost glowed.

Thank heavens she wasn't thinking abortion, Elena thought. She respected the major decision.

"But, here's the kicker," Britni announced, rising and pacing in front of them. She hesitated with deliberation, opening her mouth and then closing it with such determination that her even teeth clicked. "I want you two to raise it." A heavy calm invaded the twelve-by-twelve foot room. "What do you think?" Her look, focused on Hunt, didn't betray any shame.

"You're not serious?" His expression could be classified in the shock-and-awe category.

At the same time, waves of both terror and cheer swept through Elena. Even though she was honored, taking on this responsibility would be in total disharmony with her desired lifestyle. With a baby in the mix, adjustment would be one thing, but raising it quite a radical concept.

"I know this is all new—and I didn't mean to spring it on you like this—but I had no other way." She talked rapidly and used animated hand gestures. Her eyes were bright and the color in her cheeks darkened. Even now, her pride hadn't gone out of style.

As Elena listened, she detected no note of resentment. Disgrace didn't enter the picture either. In the course of the conversation, a healthy debate ensued.

"I'm totally serious about giving you the baby." Britni returned to the couch. "I haven't yet worked out the details, of course, but I know in my heart where the baby belongs." She let loose with an expressive shrug.

"Um . . . um . . ." Hunt started, but couldn't finish. With apparent reluctance, he chose not to scorn. The deed was done.

What more could be said?

On the other hand, Elena's spirits lifted. This might work out! This could be her chance to finally be a mother! Just when her heart could use a rest, it would instead be energized with a godsend in unknown proportions.

Oh, how the universe worked in extraordinary ways.

If only she were a fortune-teller and could foresee the future.

"Obviously, we're stunned." Elena blinked with might while a strange and peculiar surge worked through her system. "It's going to take time to wrap our heads around your news and figure out the next step."

"I understand. And . . . I'm truly sorry." Those imminent tears began their journey. The girl rushed from the room without further word.

Elena had never seen her cry. What a revelation. Yet she had to wonder if, after she had given birth, Britni would truly put aside all claims to the baby. Would she walk away and carry on with her life even as the child became a family member? Although her manifestation was admirable, she could change her mind at any time.

In the approaching interval to come, this development would demand attention. The coming months would turn into times of plans, hopes, fears, and inevitable problems. Elena's world would be affected no matter the outcome.

Once again.

Right now, all she and Hunt could do was stare at one another in disbelief. Each seemed wrapped up in her or his individual thoughts, or maybe even dreams.

Breathe in.

Hold.

Breathe out.
Repeat.
Peace.

***

A stubborn silence pulsed through the room. Elena rested her head against the back of the couch.

"Why, oh why, did this have to happen to us?" Hunt said, massaging his temples. The confession had staggered him. "Didn't I tell you just a minute ago that we'd have more complications?" Irritation and alarm worked hard against each other. "Damn it!"

He was thirsty, but the soda did no good when he took a drink.

However much Hunt might have felt disposed toward confidence, he, too, was astounded by the news. "I thought maybe I was hearing wrong. That the pain pills were doing a number on me," he told Elena.

Some inhibition seemed to be binding him closely to polite dialogue.

He shut his eyes and tunneled through all of Britni's information. He was the kind of man who wanted facts served up in clear, plain style, and right now, he wasn't getting all of those. Yet he kept his cool.

With a bit of luck, perhaps his granddaughter would have a change of heart and give the child away. That would solve everyone's problems.

It seemed the only solution. He wasn't cut out to start another new family.

No way!

Not again. Not at his age.

What was she thinking?

"I just can't believe it," he said. "What timing. Decker's on probation, I had an accident, you need to get to a doctor, you're moving your office . . ." He listed the misfortunes in a cynical tone.

Muffled thumping from Britni's music resounded down the hallway.

"Here I take them in as a favor to not only their mom but also to their dad." He talked as if to himself. "And this is how it turns out." He glanced at his watch.

"Well, it didn't happen under our roof," Elena replied. She fidgeted with a strand of hair.

"Regardless, it happened." He propped himself up more in the chair. "Simply another case in point: People don't always take the best option available," he said, referring to Britni. "Sometimes I feel these kids are strangers to me." He exhaled a deep sigh. Now they had to live with one more consequence, one more major struggle.

The guilt he carried could not have been extinguished with a strong fire hose.

Deep in contemplation, he didn't dare ask himself: What next?

COMING TO TERMS

Fresh from her confession, Britni studied her features in front of the dresser mirror in her bedroom. Nibbling on her thumbnail, she shook her head as if she were brandishing a weapon that could scare away a nagging headache and pent-up uncertainty.

Swiveling right, then left, she noticed her puffy face and bulging waistline. Because she'd always dressed so trendily, she was trying to figure out how she could disguise her changing appearance at school by wearing certain outfits.

To a teenage girl, plumping up was a major deal. A noticeable one if approached incorrectly.

How much longer could she hide her pregnancy and weight gain? Fool others?

Normally weighing in at 115 pounds, she wondered what her final number would be on her delivery day. Recently, she'd taken to eating salads and very little else. The act hadn't escaped Elena's notice, but she hadn't caught on to the reason until tonight.

She'd purchased a spandex girdle two months ago, realizing it would become a staple in her wardrobe. In theory, the scheme of wearing it sounded great. Yet in reality, she knew it would be in vain.

Thank goodness football season was over; even so, basketball had just begun. Being a cheerleader, she couldn't sustain the false front for more than a couple of more weeks. So far, she'd hidden her secret well and had no intention of abandoning her image in the remote future.

Should I take an Instagram picture now? she asked herself. *Before I get any bigger?* Ironically, her phone pinged with one coming in. The screen showed a group of her friends using Hula-Hoops, a form of exercise they all swore by for a skinnier waist. What a laugh! She had passed on their invitation to join them, thinking the action may hurt the baby.

Sooner or later, she'd have to make crucial changes or else arouse suspicion. Her classmates weren't stupid, and situations like this weren't uncommon. She knew she'd get bullied—that's just the way it was no matter what the experts strived for.

Pacing back and forth, she wrapped her arms around herself, contemplating the future. Decker was sworn to secrecy and her best friend, Gemma Myles, also knew about the circumstances, but she'd given her word she'd remain silent. As of an hour ago, her grandfather and Elena had joined the circle of trusted advocates. She hoped they would all become closer to her.

She'd heard that people sometimes do when a secret is involved.

She knew she'd have to tell her own parents at some point. Her mom was still so fragile; she didn't want to add to her troubles. News like this could set back her progress. Then again, maybe she wouldn't have to find out until after the fact.

Britni's dad had been so proud of her up to now. She was his first child and she prayed that with the news, he'd continue to feel pleased with her. College was still an aspiration. She wasn't going to let that plan slip away if at all possible. A four-year theatrical concentration at Ohio University had been her goal for two years now.

This stumbling block shouldn't alter the objective. She'd have the baby, finish high school, enjoy the summer, and then be off to Athens, Ohio, come the middle of August.

She sat at the bureau, which was littered with toiletries and hair accessories, and brushed her long, thick ebony locks over her shoulder. Today, it was her natural color. The night she became pregnant it had been blue—a rather sapphire tone. She put down the brush and closed her eyes, recounting the moments leading up to that particular turning point.

One Saturday in late June, her dad had let her go to a college pool party. She and Gemma had met some freshman guys who were taking summer classes in town at Central State University. The girls lied about how old they were and, managing to pull off the maturity act, the guys invited them to a fraternity bash.

During the festivities, Britni had cozied up to a six-foot buffed blond dude dressed in the style that attracted her. Cal Hudson wore the latest trend of cargo shorts, short-sleeved Henley shirt, and slip-on boat shoes. She had imagined he would look straight-fire in a suit, too. Adding to his impressive resumé was the eagle tattoo on his left forearm.

She had been more than enthralled.

They chatted for a while, each showing interest in the other. She had learned about some of his courses, where he came from, a few of his hobbies. He discovered she loved to shop, that nothing could be done to control her interest in clothes. Plus, that she'd been an honor student upon graduation (which was a fabrication), and that she'd been to numerous concerts (which was also a lie).

After hours of drinking and a few hits of pot, all the guests went swimming in the host's in-ground pool. As the night wore on, several of the guests departed, even Gemma, who had monopolized a freckle-faced intellectual's time. She'd no doubt refer to him as her bae the next day, Britni was sure of it. Her best friend had been just like that since grade school.

Sure enough, she didn't disappoint the following day.

Finding themselves to be the last two left in the pool, Britni and Cal initiated the make-out routine. Neither could fight the mutual attraction and soon they were doing the nasty right there in some family's professionally landscaped backyard.

Although Britni couldn't remember every small detail, that experience had been the most profound in her life to date. Still an apprentice at intimacy, she had felt so mature and adult.

At present, she rifled through a pile of clothes stacked at the foot of her bed. She selected a pair of black leggings and a long top for school tomorrow. Discreet and stylish, she could get by with it for the time being. However, it was only October. She would just continue to gain more weight. What was she going to do?

In the days ahead, would her popularity plummet? Or would the kids admire her courage?

She'd soon find out.

No matter what, in the next slow-going five months, she'd refuse to be ashamed or embarrassed. Britni Klyce wasn't made to buckle under that kind of intimidation.

She smoothed down a plum-colored handkerchief dress and gingerly placed it on the bed. Still, her mind wouldn't let up on that summer episode. It wasn't her only sexual encounter; nevertheless, it was the only one with an older guy and the only one without protection. Through Facebook and chat, she'd found out that Cal had a steady girlfriend back home and wasn't keen on breaking that bond. Which was fine by her; she wasn't heartbroken over it. She carried on and enjoyed the rest of the season at her dad's, turning eighteen in July.

It was five weeks after the pool party that morning sickness, two a missed periods, frequent trips to the bathroom, and a sensitivity to the smell of grease led to the realization she was pregnant. The positive results from those over-the-counter tests sealed her fate.

Now she was at a crossroads, trying to concentrate on her classes and aiming to keep her spirits up. One resolution she'd maintained since she'd learned about the pregnancy was that she would deliver the baby. In what may be the most difficult decision of her life so far, she'd concluded there would be no abortion, and no adoption if it could be helped.

That's when she had the idea of Granddad and Elena keeping the child as their own. This family needed some kind of permanent bond. It had been shattered way too long.

In the end, would the older couple go through with it? Abide by her request?

What if they didn't? That would definitely shift the landscape of her life. She bit her lip at the prospect—not to mention the gamble.

Her phone pinged again. This time it was a message about her cheerleading practice tomorrow after school. It was the last thing she felt like doing, yet she had to maintain normalcy for the time being.

Her headache had deepened to a dull, heavy frontal pain—almost blinding. She opened the window for a breath of fresh air. The sun had recently set and a gaggle of geese flew over, honking in unison. She giggled at the noise. If only she could join them and escape to the skies with no worries to be had.

Peering at the orangey glow of the horizon, she thought back to Elena and her reaction to the news. The woman had been so sweet and kind to her at the disclosure. She possessed a hidden strength Britni was oddly jealous of.

In fact, that was the number one factor leading her decision to turn over the baby. She knew Elena Polson would make an excellent mother. True, she was a tad bit quirky in her personality and direct approaches, but deep down, Britni admired those traits too. Although she'd never admit it to others.

With her generation's craving for instant gratification, she didn't understand Elena's preoccupation with thinking things through. The woman was over-the-top conscientious. It seemed to just be her nature. And to Britni's amazement, the woman managed to pull off her thrift-store fashions in good taste. She certainly knew how to pinch a penny. No wonder Granddad cherished her.

Like for the dance last spring, when she suggested Britni wear Doretta's special dress. The whole look had made her feel extraordinary. Once she'd slipped on the vintage silk beauty in the attic that first time, she knew Elena was right; it was perfect for her. So what if it was sixty years old? It wasn't as if she was about to adopt that style permanently. The total reversal of her own pattern killed it that evening.

She had been transformed from a spoiled drama queen to a rare, one-time magical princess. The girls at the celebration had raved; the guys could only gape. Many classmates had asked where she got the gown, but she never revealed the details. Scores of kids had even Instagrammed her for the creativity. In fact, she'd received more attention than Kelli, the crowned queen of the spring dance. To this day, Kelli never let Britni forget how she'd upstaged her.

And due to the cool temperatures that special night, she'd decided to wear the mink wrap Elena recommended. Even though the fabric was scratchy, the jacket had been the precisely perfect addition to an already-gala appearance.

All in all, she had her grandfather's partner to thank for such a remarkable occasion. One she'd wished for, for ages.

She closed the window and searched through her phone pictures and found the one of that evening. She grew a smile. She'd never looked so beautiful. Kurt Mozell had shown his appreciation for choosing him as her date by screwing her in the backseat later on. Amazingly, the dress hadn't wrinkled from the exploit.

She had never once considered throwing the treasured heirloom on top of the already-mounting pile of clothing and had promptly returned it to Elena. It was now back in its designated home, hanging in the Morton's attic along with the mink wrap.

Goodness, how life had changed since that momentous occasion. Sighing, she realized that to this day she was still an apprentice at intimacy.

Her phone rang. Gemma. Britni ignored the call, choosing to keep her thoughts company instead.

She lay on the bed, bolstered up by an arrangement of pillows in a variety of sizes. Happily, the throbbing in her head had diminished. With eyes shut, she wrung her hands and sent up a prayer that Granddad and Elena would someday get married. If they decided to keep the baby, they would need to be accountable to one another because the child would need stability—and mostly, Britni longed for assurance.

All would be great. In a perfect world.

Suddenly, the baby kicked. It was the third time in recent days and she knew the sensation would become more regular from now on. She likened the feeling to a goldfish swimming inside her.

She located her ear buds and iPod and tuned in to some classic rock for inspiration. She'd come to love the genre thanks to Elena, who her mind still concentrated on.

Britni thought with regret about how she and Decker had been designedly cruel to Elena, making her life miserable. Knowing that Elena took every criticism to heart, she began to speculate whether the woman truly ragged them all that much. Could it be that they'd misinterpreted her as she tried to calm them down?

To be fair, the intention was to have their grandfather to themselves. He was someone they could rely on unconditionally and steadfastly, as they could with no one else. Whatever love was, she and Decker wanted it just like anyone did. With Elena in the mix, Hunt's allegiance could stretch only so far. And so she stood in their way.

Their mother wasn't equipped to handle them, and their biological father's responsibility was to his new clan. Grandma Gwen was eight states away, so she was not an option for escape. And Grandma Lyla had health problems. So there were no other family members to rely on.

As the eldest of the Klyce children, Britni had tried to protect Decker from their mother's emotional dependence on them. It was a tough role to fit into. When Jony *did* show affection toward them, in most cases she was high, so it was a false devotion.

Shreds of faith and little sprouts of hope led the way whenever her mom seemed to be making headway. Maybe this time, or another time, she'd finally get her shit together. Every so often, Britni served as the adult, Jony the teenager.

At least Elena wasn't like that.

However, she also wasn't her mother.

And Britni needed her mom so badly; had for many years. They were missing out on so much.

Sad to say, some things weren't meant to be.

She quickly removed the ear buds and started organizing the heaping pyramid of clothes. She didn't actually wear everything she bought. Just then, an epiphany enveloped her. She counted on the garments to make her feel good. Collecting them had served as one of her coping mechanisms.

She stared at the heap. Ridiculous as it seemed, it resembled her life so far, representing all the layers of emotions. The fear, the joy, the rebellion, the optimism, and the emptiness.

Nonetheless, she couldn't dwell on those feelings. She must look forward and develop a plan for the next few months. In a strange way, she wanted to make Elena, of all people, proud of her. Wanted to be able to give the woman something she'd never had. Perhaps it was because of guilt over the way she'd treated her. Heavens, what a way to do it by giving her a child!

Tightening her lips, she tackled the clothes and began consolidating them into the already-bulging closet. Her change of spirit, and the neatness, delighted her. Now was the time to grow a backbone and mature into an adult.

If she could bear a child, she could acquire housekeeping skills.

Right, Elena?

An aroma of vegetable soup crept under the door. It sickened her but at the same time made her stomach growl in hunger. She became cognizant of the fact she hadn't eaten all day, which wasn't good for the baby.

Momentarily, she thought about the unborn child she carried. Was it a boy or a girl? Would it have any health problems? Most importantly, would it be attractive? Straight or gay? And if Granddad and Elena adopted the baby, would it be a great uncle or great aunt to her? Or a cousin?

Or simply a stranger?

Except for the last questions, were these issues what every expectant mother deliberated with caution and full conscience?

A rap on the door startled her.

"Dinner'll be ready shortly." Elena's words filtered through the closed door.

"Okay, be right out."

Catching her reflection once more in the mirror, Britni Klyce leaned forward, wet her pinky finger, and smoothed down her eyebrows. She refused to frown.

From here on out, she promised herself she'd make up for every wrongdoing against others and make a positive metamorphosis toward gratitude. Although she'd be fortified against the odds, she'd comply by the rules set before her.

After all, they'd be a part of her future no matter the circumstances.

AT LOOSE ENDS

After her doctor's appointment five weeks later, Elena set out for Paddy's Wagon. She wanted to catch Hunt before he went to see Jony for their weekly visit.

The biggest decision of her life loomed large and was in need of discussion.

The December sky, threatening snow any minute, beckoned with crackled clouds to accompany her on the 3.6-mile journey. She had the car's heater set on medium. Driving with involuntary effort, the words from the gynecologist gave her total recall.

"Your stress level is high," Doctor Hammel had said. "You need to find a way to bring it down. Aside from meditation. Or else we'll be dealing with much more serious medical issues."

The unforeseen and surprising warning was like a foot out to trip her. Yet powerful. She had agreed right away.

She'd left the physician's office with the recommended title of a best-selling book on relaxation and mindfulness. If only her schedule allowed for concentrated reading!

Once she learned she had no impending health problems, she knew what she had to do. Find Hunt.

She'd weighed the pros and cons of legally adopting Britni's baby. She refused any alternatives but doing the honorable thing. The true resolution for all concerned.

Did she trust herself enough to carry this through?

Pulling in to the parking lot of the tavern, she mentally geared up for the ensuing resistance from Hunt. She shut off the car and bundled up. The cold grayness of an early winter had a depressing effect on her spirit.

Exiting the car, she hurried to the entrance. She stopped with a hand on the door as apprehension guest-starred on her emotional stage. Hunt's understanding of this important life-changing arrangement was paramount. She had to persuade him to get on board or else none of it would work. The choice couldn't be all her own; it would take both of them. Right now, she needed him as a safeguard more than ever.

She'd wasted enough time on automatic pilot throughout the years, the course of her life was past due to change. And becoming a bona fide parent would be the biggest transformation to date.

Confidence possessed her and she forged into the lobby. A country ballad engulfed the air while smoke rose and became part of the ceiling, much like a haze settling over a mountain. She glanced around the familiar, obscure atmosphere for Hunt.

In the past, she'd nurtured many a Chablis hangover after being here.

She noticed a sprinkling of people at the counter and then spotted him seated at a booth with three other men she recognized as part of his work team. They were in a barroom huddle, no doubt discussing their jobs. The three men had questions on their faces, whereas Hunt's was animated around his neat and trimmed goatee. He was tilted back in his chair, the picture of a man who had been victorious in a crisis. And, he was drinking a cup of coffee. Not his regular glass of Jack Daniels.

He'd kept his promise to her. This was one of the moments she adored him.

When she approached, the ensemble didn't immediately acknowledge her because they were engrossed in their deep, stimulating conversation.

Then Hunt looked up, quick with his smile. "Hey, hon!" He patted the empty seat beside him and the men scooted closer together to make room for her.

"Hi, all!" she said.

One man halfway rose out of his seat in respect, while another toasted his glass toward her. The last tipped his head and cigarette. All gentlemen. There were still some left.

"We were just discussing the ISIS terrorist situation and how we could solve the problem," Hunt informed her, rubbing his chin.

She took a seat. "Did you come up with anything conclusive?" she asked, knowing she intruded on their sanctuary. She coughed from the pollution.

"I did," said the guy with a pockmarked complexion as he played with the sweat on his whiskey glass. "I say they all go back to where they came from and everybody minds their own business, including us. It worked in the old days, it can work now."

"I'm with you," she said, her conscience eased. She placed her hands on the sticky surface of the tabletop. This wasn't a place for cloth napkins and leather menus.

He nodded toward the others. "See? Told ya someone would agree with me."

A spot of classic rock music filled the air. It was as rich and vibrant as a Spanish guitar.

"Want a drink?" Hunt asked her.

She wrung her hands. "No, I'm good." A strong whiff of French-fry grease coasted through the room. "Hunt, I need to talk to you." She lowered her voice. "It's important." She wasted no strokes.

He patted her hand, now at her lap. "Sure," he said loudly. "I can't solve the world's problems here, so I might as well go home."

A round of chuckling invaded their space.

He fished in his pocket and threw a few dollars onto the table. "Well, fellas, we're outta here." He stood and edged away, helping her do the same. "See ya tomorrow!"

She waved to the crew as Hunt hovered by her side. "Bye, guys."

They took their leave and Hunt steered her, his hand at her elbow, to the exit. "You okay?"

"Fine. Just need some alone time."

Outside, an unexpected keen wind met them when they came around the corner of the building on their way to his rental truck. "Brrr, get in," he instructed upon reaching the vehicle. They scrambled onto the front leather seat. He started the engine and adjusted the heat to the highest level, then he threw a glance toward her, clapping his gloved palms together. "Now, what's so important?" A shadow crossed his face. "Was it something the doctor said? Should I be concerned?"

She grinned. "Actually, I'm good to go. The report was positive, and as long as I find a way to reduce my stress somehow, I'll be even better."

He kissed her cheek and exhaled with intention. "Thank goodness!" He slipped an arm around her shoulders. "We'll figure it out. Together."

The rest of the world fell away in that moment.

Although Elena wouldn't classify herself as being exuberant, she felt more excited than she had ever been. With the baby, she would have someone to love unconditionally besides a parent or sister, like Hunt already had with his kids and grandkids. *A person with no baggage—not somebody I'd covet for recognition,* she thought, recalling her father's temperament.

This rapport would be a clean-cut road in which to shape another human being into her fold. Anticipation combated fear, each emotion preceding restlessness.

"Hunt, I want to keep the baby." She tensed, plunging into a discussion of her plans. "I realize how hard it's going to be, especially on our relationship." She felt fragile, as if she walked through a china shop with guarded movements. "But this is my chance, my opportunity to be a mother."

Since that day of Britni's declaration, they had danced around the probability, never discussing the girl's idea at any length. And now the pregnancy was in its sixth month.

In the old days, this type of situation would have qualified for a scandal.

Elena focused on Hunt's profile, trying to predict his true feelings. Would he accept the fantastic implications? Or would he relieve himself of the responsibilities?

Without delay, he broke away and frowned her into silence. "Why? Why do you want to take on that obligation?" He stared into space. "Don't we have enough problems?" His voice dripped in woe. "If you'll forgive me, we aren't young. Far from it."

The minutes ticked by and seemed like years. A few snowflakes pecked at the windshield and the sky darkened. In her current state, she couldn't let her bargaining power slip away. Even though her emotions mimicked a frayed cloth with uncut lines.

"A chance like this only comes along once for me. And I want it so badly!" Tears formed and threatened to make their journey. "Please, Hunt?" Her speech only carried so far in the still air.

The breath he inhaled was loud. "I admire your courage, baby. I really do." He shrank against the door as if he'd overheard her reflections. "But I just don't see how we could be any good as parents." In the dim illumination, his grim face showcased. "So far, we've been lousy grandparents."

She deemed the words appropriate, but she didn't want to be on the losing side of this exchange.

The snowfall became heavier, coating the ground. Daylight was well done for this particular Wednesday. She shivered at the weather, and at the thought of his potential refusal. Would this impasse be their final demise?

"We'll just have to learn not to repeat the same mistakes," she cried.

He shifted uneasily in his seat and his eyes grew wide. "Is this *really* what you want? You're willing to give up your freedom?" He shook his head. "Besides, you just said you need to cut down on stress. And something like this is worlds away from a solution." He played with the steering wheel. "Have you thought this through? All the way through?"

"Yes!" She had projected his questions. "But it would be a wonderful kind of stress. Hunt, I also know I'd be a great mother. And you'd have a second chance at being a wonderful father, to continue that love into the next generation." She squeezed his hand. "One we would have control of," she urged. "You and me."

The profound burps of a neighboring pickup's loud engine interrupted the tranquility. The odor of diesel whirled out of its exhaust.

Why must there always be a distraction? she wondered. *Even with just the two of us alone in a damn parking lot?*

"But . . . but won't it drain your energy? How would you have stamina left for *us*?" He furrowed his brow, his look enveloping distress. "I don't want to lose that." He took her hand to reiterate his point.

"I understand all your concerns, believe me. This wasn't easy for me, either." She tilted her head and played with a strand of hair. "But I've never wanted anything more in my life. Ever." She emphasized the last word and prayed it didn't complicate the situation further.

Another bout of quietness deluged the car's interior. The thunderous truck had since departed.

"Nothing comes free, my dear." His words infiltrated the hush. "Even consequences."

She was quick with a response. "My, that's a strange thing to say." In that unguarded moment, tears made an appearance.

He snickered. "I've had lots of practice to be able to say it." He turned his head to look out the driver's side window. His breath steamed up the glass. "Plus, I still contend that the less we think about the future, the better for our nerves." He was all about the present.

This sudden application of cold logic startled her. At this juncture, she didn't know if she faced success or defeat.

He rotated back around to face her and her eyes bore into his. Hunt's expression suggested he was planning a con job. "Irony is a damn funny thing, isn't it?" He let loose with one of his infectious winks.

The love between them was once again tested.

"So, you'll at least think about it?" Her foot involuntarily tapped against the floorboard. "Britni hasn't said a word about changing her mind on us taking the baby; and she's due in three months. She needs an answer." Her heart beat in a pitter-patter, anticipating his feedback.

"There's no doubt you'd be a great mother." He caressed her thigh and blushed. "Of that, I am sure."

With that statement, Elena's mind raced with possibilities. There was plenty of life left for plans.

"Thank you." Her anxiety immediately lowered by at least two degrees. "I needed to hear that." She snuggled into his neck and noted the clock on the dashboard. "You'd better get to Jony's before the weather gets any worse."

He nodded. "I know." He kissed her forehead.

"We'll talk later." She felt like she had claimed a small victory.

Just as she opened the door, he caught her arm. "I do love you." He blinked heavily. "So much. And I will think about this, I promise."

"That's all I ask." She rescued a smile. "Love you, too. Be careful."

Back in her SUV, she steadied her shaking body.

Inhale.

Hold.

Exhale.

Harmony.

Where would she be without her meditation?

She didn't want to think about it.

***

Eleven days later, the first day of the Christmas holiday for the kids, Brent Dorsey stepped up to the plate and decided to take full legal custody of his son Decker. All involved knew they would be good for one another.

Britni would stay behind with Hunt and Elena and graduate from high school in May.

Interesting how things work out or how prayers are answered, thought Elena. But, most important of all, Hunt relented to Elena's request.

In those following days, he'd gone from negativity to compromise then to final, reluctant surrender, concluding that adopting the baby would indeed be best for everyone concerned. With love and dedication, they would find a way to manage the trials and tribulations ahead.

It was the best Christmas Elena Polson could remember in a very, very long time.

***

Shortly after the introduction of the new year, Elena and Hunt made an appointment with an attorney specializing in child custody. The first step in their new beginning.

Life was looking up.

Way up.

ONE BETTER

"I'm ready." The words came from Britni as she stood over Elena and Hunt's bed before sunrise on the fourteenth of February. Valentine's Day.

Elena took a moment to awaken. "Ready for what?"

Hunt was snoring in a light tone.

"Um, the baby's ready." The girl switched on the light. Her face was drawn and pale as she grabbed her forty-inch waist.

Elena fumbled with the covers, and consciousness. "Okay, give us a minute!" She nudged Hunt awake as Britni left the room.

This was it. *The* day. The major juncture in her life. Her emotional repertoire began to take shape.

Would she become a mother today? Or would Britni change her mind and want the baby?

Elena and Hunt hurried to get themselves together. Ten minutes later, they were all out the door. On the way to the SUV, Britni stopped in her tracks several times, understandably in pain. Her grandfather helped her into the car.

The ride to the hospital was quiet. Hunt drove because he'd rehearsed this drive on more than one occasion recently. Britni managed to subdue her moans, but her white-knuckled hands clenched the door armrest and the console on either side of her.

"I'm so proud of you," Elena said from the backseat. "You are so brave." Her optimism gained momentum alongside the sweat on her palms. Was she worked up for herself, or for Britni? Or both? "Just hang on a little longer." *No pun intended.*

Hunt checked the time on the dash. "About four more minutes, sweetie. We'll make it." He patted his granddaughter's knee.

They arrived at the hospital's emergency entrance and Elena hightailed it to the first person on staff she saw to assist Britni to the appropriate place. Within minutes, off she went in a wheelchair.

"We'll catch up!" Elena called after them. She proceeded to the registration desk while Hunt parked. Steadying herself against the counter, she provided the applicable information. A tingle of excitement worked up her spine.

From there, she found Hunt in the chilly waiting room. It was empty except for them. A flood of fluorescent lighting engulfed the space.

Britni had wanted no family with her when she delivered and they abided by her request. She also stipulated that she didn't want to know the sex of the baby until it was born.

They spoke little as Hunt paced back and forth along the two-toned gray laminate floor. Elena smiled at him, at the man who was her emotional reinforcement. The one she knew would take care of her and the baby from now on.

If that was indeed the case.

What a monumental day!

Never mind the past and all the adversity she'd endured. It was time to put it behind.

An eternity later—two hours and fifty-one minutes to be exact—a nurse summoned them to the post-delivery room. Elena's mindset was a kaleidoscope of feelings looping around from fear to happiness to panic.

This day would forever be ingrained in her memory.

Britni's features were surprisingly vibrant as she lay in her bed. Had she really just given birth to a child? Even now, she knew how to appear her best.

"It's a girl," she announced as a nurse checked her vitals.

Butterflies leaped around Elena's stomach. She'd have a little girl to raise as her own. *Won't I?* "That's wonderful . . . have you seen her?" She tried to tone down her enthusiasm, which was leaving its mark through her body.

So this is what it's like to be a new parent? To discover you've brought a new being into the world?

In the meantime, Hunt sat at Britni's side, sporting a proud grin. Somewhere in the distance, a faint ambulance siren heralded.

"For a second," Britni responded, taking in a deep breath. "From what they told me, I had an easy labor." Her eyes shone crystal clear. "I have to admit, she's beautiful." She shifted within the bed and rotated her neck.

Elena joined them at bedside. "What a relief. You did so good, sweetie!" She put sympathy in her words.

"Yes, she did." The words came from the doorway, from Jony Klyce. She entered the room.

"Mom!" Tears reserved only for a chosen few in Britni's world made their appearance. "But . . . but . . ." She was clearly astounded.

Hunt rose and hugged his daughter. "I promised not to tell anyone, and I didn't," he confessed. "No one."

He winked at Elena. She held back, flabbergasted but pleased. She would soon be a part of this family, no matter the outcome of today. Her dry mouth scraped her tongue, not realizing until now that she hadn't eaten anything since last night.

Those butterflies could very well have been hunger, too.

With a wide grin, Jony made her way to Britni. She was dressed in a slim-fitting tangerine T-shirt over worn jeans, appearing healthy and strong. If this scene were to be watched in fifties black-and-white, Jony would easily pass for a Susan Hayward look-alike. The high cheekbones, chic mid-length hairstyle, and perfect figure gave her that whimsical appearance. If she could just maintain that aura through full recovery, Elena was confident she'd eventually find her way to successful healing.

"Hey, baby girl," Jony said. "How was it?" She brushed back Britni's hair from her face.

How could anyone who didn't know her circumstances believe she had stability problems? Because by mere observation, she exuded normalcy.

"It wasn't as bad as I thought, Mom." Her voice was gravelly as she held her mother's hand. "But I have no intention of repeating it anytime soon."

The room filled with laughter.

"Was it a boy, or a girl?" Jony asked. She smiled in admiration.

"Girl. Her name is Seda Allison Klyce," Britni informed everyone as a dramatic smile brightened her expression.

The other request she'd had about the whole ordeal, besides delivering the baby alone not knowing its sex, was to name it. Elena wasn't thrilled with her choice of name, but the teen had given her and Hunt a new foundation, a new life. How could they begrudge her that wish?

"Did you tell them yet?" Jony asked Britni.

Hunt responded first. "Tell us what?"

Now who was keeping a secret?

"Dad, Elena—Britni's coming home with me." It seemed Jony had saved enough money from a job as a case-management assistant at the facility to rent a two-bedroom apartment in the same school district as theirs.

It was clear there were new starts for everyone. Pride lent credence to this alliance.

The announcement was short-lived as a woman from the hospital's legal office interrupted their visit. She wore eyeglasses atop her red hair and a deadpan look.

"Sorry, folks, but I need to talk to a"—she surveyed a page from the clipboard—" Hunt Klyce and Elena Polson." She spoke the words in a brusque, businesslike manner.

"That's us." Instantly, Elena's and Britni's eyes locked into a reassuring gaze, meant only for the two of them.

Britni crinkled her eyes and nose and nodded. At the same time, Elena beamed.

The time had arrived. Everything she'd known changed at exactly 11:36 a.m. A sense of security closed in. Till this very moment, Elena's uncertainty about Britni's decision had remained paramount. Not her job, not her relationship, not anything else.

By that very gesture seconds before, Britni had given Elena and Hunt permission to take over the legalities of adoption. According to this lady standing before them, Britni had already and without hesitation signed the necessary documents, waiving all rights to the child. Relinquishing Seda to her grandfather and his life partner.

All she wanted was to finish high school and embark on a college education. Both were very important to her. No, this setback wouldn't deter

Britni Klyce. She had a bright future ahead of her; she was still full of hope and determination.

In spite of everything, Elena had to wonder if she had ever contacted the baby's father. Knowing her as she did, the chances were slim, given the complexity of the matter.

It wouldn't have changed anything anyhow.

Elena and Hunt left Britni and Jony to their reunion and followed the official to her office.

"Are you sure about this?" Hunt asked her on the way, holding her hand. "Positive?"

She carved out a smile, hoping it relayed her answer. "Definitely."

She pulled her nerves together and they signed the forms in all the proper places. For a split second, Hunt seemed to hesitate. This was a major decision for him, too.

Afterward, they headed to the delivery room. Seda was one of three other babies in their individual incubators. Her eyes were open, perhaps to signal a hello to her new parents, and that she was ready for their love. And their world.

Hunt slipped an arm around Elena's waist. "There's your daughter, my love."

"Oh, how I delight in the sound of that." Her tears were warm on her face and she was powerless to stop them. Meanwhile, a fresh complacency gave her a shakedown.

Seda Allison Klyce smiled on one side of the glass while the grown-ups kissed on the other.

Each of their lives was intact and forever changed on this particular Valentine's Day.

AND BABY MAKES FIVE

Two months later, early spring made a grand entrance with blooming flowers and days upon end of doting sunshine. One bright April day, Elena looked out her sister's attic window onto the green and yellow scene. Startling her, the resident cardinal flew onto the outside sill.

She pecked at the glass with her finger to signal her presence to the bird. It didn't fly off but just looked at her and ruffled its feathers. Elena grinned and took a moment to think back to her follow-up doctor appointment ten days ago. She'd found out that her hormones were in need of regulating and she was prescribed the correct treatment. The almost-instant positive change in her temperament, along with an escalation of meditation, had made a difference in her stamina.

What was left included adding better self-care and recharging elements to the equation. Because now she was a mother and required all the energy and patience she could find.

Today, for some inexplicable reason, she felt as lighthearted and as fresh as a breeze might over a seashore. She turned and glanced at the sleeping two-month-old baby in her bassinet only three feet away. She cocked her head in bliss.

Seda Allison Klyce was *her* two-month-old baby by surrogacy.

Eleven pounds, three ounces of undisputed fascination, along with ample facial cheeks, a full head of brown hair, healthy pale-white skin, and a disposition of spunky proportions. Much like her biological mother.

Elena inched over to the crib and lightly touched the baby's pink cheek in mellow admiration. "My little Valentine." She couldn't wait to raise Seda with old-fashioned values, manners, and responsibilities to the best of her knowledge.

In the twenty-first century, the venture would no doubt be phenomenal and complicated. However, the possibilities gave her cause to shiver in joy. This child would keep her young in spirit and attitude.

The bird at the window tweeted and was soon joined by a companion. They began a duet. Elena wondered if the act was for her and Seda's benefit. Two by two, a bonded duo, together they would unite. Within minutes, the two feathered friends took flight.

She sat in an antique rocker and continued processing some recent events. In particular, the marriage proposal from Hunt last week and his promise to stop drinking for the most part. Both developments put a firm grasp on her future.

When she and Hunt had first met up, she was an independent and carefree woman who had settled for a wayward lifestyle. But he had changed her, for the better. She had resisted the urge to live in a vacuum long enough.

Allowing herself a little self-pity, she had learned that immortal lesson of what it takes to be a member of a family. It was almost as if she had been spinning on a merry-go-round and the Klyces had pushed her faster and faster. And there was no stopping it.

Till now.

Lesson learned.

Through her tenure, were these the answers she'd been seeking in the interim?

Did she get what she deserved?

Had the baby been in the nick of time, saving her before she hit rock bottom?

Every question integrated awareness as she had reinvented herself along the way. And now, she could add courage to her emotional resumé.

Without warning, the neighbor's cocker spaniel began barking. Elena hoped it wouldn't wake up Seda. She heard another dog call out in answer. She shook her head in amazement and stretched her neck.

To be sure, she'd landed in uncharted territory: a middle-aged explorer in a far-off world. Yet she had also added an army of committed loved ones. Even Decker had signed on for cousin duty, elated at having someone to love without conditions.

She snickered.

Living with his father and changing schools had allowed Decker to make great strides. As luck would have it, he'd started working at the humane society by the judge's orders. He enjoyed it and had learned to love animals and to care for them properly. Plus, Brent's wife had forgiven him for the accident many months ago.

Decker was in good hands and in good shape. A place he needed to be.

Scribes had been arrested again. He and his brothers had robbed a convenience store. Some people are just destined to be, and cause, trouble.

Seda twitched in her sleep and cooed. It wouldn't be long until she was awake.

Elena had brought her here to infuse her with sentimentality and the importance of heritage. Where better place than the one overflowing with ancestral prominence, the one where she had found solace throughout the years?

She took in another quiet internalizing moment before her daughter would require attention.

Until now, she hadn't seen that life had the potential for more inspiration. Obsessing with the past and dealing with discouragement had almost been a part-time career, one with no values.

Had she finally made it?

Would the baby be her answer? Bring her the joy she so desperately craved?

Through the floorboards, she heard Pidge rustling around. She would join them soon.

The baby cried out and Elena retrieved the full bottle of formula from the corner of the cradle. As she held her new daughter in her arms and fed the child, her heart spread its wings. She knew there would be many more precious moments like this to come.

A tear rolled down her cheek as Seda smiled at her from the garnet-colored hand-me-down crocheted blanket she was nestled in. From here on out, the sacrifice was Elena's long-term contract. She had crossed over into a love without end; a security no one would confiscate.

Was this the same feeling most new mothers experienced?

Before long, she'd have to begin a renewed mission and discover how to budget every little thing, to follow some kind of logic. In time, she was sure she'd declare this passage a milestone in her existence.

She had been a victim of her own circumstances long enough.

Last month, she had moved from the co-op and turned Britni's bedroom into her copywriting studio. She had every intention of taking on the double role of copywriter and mom. She never had complained about multi-tasking; rather, she tackled it. And this situation would definitely test that strength.

In Seda's presence, she no longer felt uncertain as to what her purpose was in that once-unfulfilled reality. The completeness held redemption. Mentally, she was in a good place. In the company of the young, no one could be depressed.

She brought the baby up to her chest and burped her. But Seda was ready for more of the drink, making her wishes known with a fuss.

She quieted her with the bottle's nipple and padded around the room. She passed the fragile mink wrap hanging in its secure spot and paused in front of it. She took Seda's little hand and rubbed the vintage fur. The baby's eyes reacted in enchantment.

She, too, was empowered by the treasure. Elena couldn't be more pleased.

Sitting in the rocker once more, continuing to nourish her baby, she took in the scent of the newborn's fragrance. The sweet body essence, the delicate scent of baby powder, the well-rounded goodness of innocence. An everlasting delight.

Sunlight began to draw a path on the wooden floor, warming the enclosed space. She checked her watch and realized it was late afternoon. Where had the time gone? It seemed she'd only been here a minute or so, but it had been close to two hours.

Much like the rays flooding the room, a sense of wonder filled her spirit as she peered down at the baby. That face full of virtue made her heart skip a beat. Even though she hadn't bore the child, the unconditional love racing through her was nothing short of wonder. How could she be so lucky?

The pitching motion of the rocker had returned Seda to slumber.

Is this what normal felt like? Elena wondered. Or what she assumed was normal for most people? If so, she loved the feeling. Although she had hardened throughout the years, she would use any redeeming wisdom to her benefit.

The ride had been anything but easy. Up to now, the world had come in stages of remnants, a patchwork plan. It seemed like she had never owned her problems, often finding that fortitude had closed up shop. And when she summoned up the recent past, she remembered the days feeling like she was driving a car, passing on a double-yellow line and not knowing the outcome.

On the other hand, with her new family, her feelings had been pried open to reveal a side of herself she had hidden away, far away. It had a tendency to expose more dignity and courage.

She'd have nothing to breathe but air from now on, although she was sure there'd be times when the journey would be like traveling in a nighttime fog with only a sole headlight as a guide. The next several months would prove to be impressive. Only a few more corners to turn and those involved would be on the right track. Steady and true.

Pidge now stood at the door and Elena ushered her into the room.

"Welcome to your new life," Pidge said. "There's no denying it, you've been reoriented." She clenched her sister's warm hand while her full face quivered, pulling at the corners of her eyes and mouth.

"About time, eh?" She handed the baby to her sister. Seda stirred awake. "She is the missing factor I couldn't figure out for myself." The confession gave her a chill. "Who would've thought?"

"She's so beautiful," Pidge said with cheer, kissing Seda's forehead. "You've made me very happy." The words were directed at the infant. "You've given me bragging rights." Last month, she had retired from her bank position and was now ready to help her sister with the transition of parenthood. She, too, had made sacrifices.

"Pidge?" Elena's insecurity made a brief appearance.

"Yes, dear?"

"Do you think she's my redemption?" In the confined space, the words sounded like a small breeze swimming around a wind chime. "My guiding spirit?"

Pidge took a moment to respond. "It's not my place to answer that, sweetheart. There's no doubt in my mind that she's a huge factor." Her pleasure grew visibly as she cradled the baby in her arms, ambling about the attic. "In fact, I'll worship this child till I die." She said it as if it were an afterthought while she swayed back and forth.

Elena snickered inwardly. *Had Britni had the child, or Pidge?*

"But fate, indeed, was on your side," Pidge added. "And time will be your friend from here on out." Her expression changed to mercy.

"Oh, I truly believe that." Elena weighed every word her only sibling spoke, her insight treasured for all time.

Taking the baby, she placed her back in the vintage wicker crib, one she had lain in herself. It was another item built to last forever. Her inheritance would remain intact, even with this new person. Tonight, right before sleep, she would play "Brahm's Lullaby" to her new daughter on her flute, just as she had every night since her birth.

The baby fell asleep straightaway every time.

Elena would make sure music became an important staple for the child.

"My personal history sure has been a gamble. And it's not that I'm not a winner, it's just that I've lost so much along the way." She fretted, changing Seda's diaper. The baby squirmed. "Age will do that to a person." Her voice grew louder and she seemed to speak more to herself than to any listener. "Who would have imagined I'd be a mother? At this juncture?"

Pidge took the dirty item and placed it on the rocker's seat. "But what more can we ask of ourselves than to raise a child?" Her speech hit the air with exuberance. "And one that isn't even our own?" she ruminated, her face serene. "It stands to reason your life has taken a huge turn. You'll have to summon up bravery from deep within."

Pidge was right. Everything considered, there would be no room for doubts and speculations. On the other hand, there would also be no more freedom or independence.

Was Elena Polson ready?

"Exactly." She covered Seda again with the blanket and her daughter cooed.

Her lifestyle would be rebuilt, structured within the parameters of parenthood. Somehow, she would find the meaning behind the word.

"Mother would have been so overjoyed." She scooped up the baby and took her to the window, embracing her with a gentle hug. The bright light made the youngster wince. "This is where you belong, Seda Allison Klyce. Always." Happy tears filled her eyes. "Don't ever forget it."

That being said, Elena could continue her history in the most paradoxical path one could imagine.

Still, new and unfamiliar concerns cluttered her mind.

She realized she would have to draw out the inner strength she had hidden deep inside and find a reason to believe. Adulthood had been irrefutably full of unpredictable ironies.

With this change, she'd have to work on that inferiority holding her back, and continue believing in faith. Now part of a majority instead of a minority, she knew appreciation would steadily deepen as guardianship took hold.

If this was exactly where she belonged, she could thank destiny.

And Britni Klyce.

The once-manipulative, shallow, and apathetic girl had transformed into a mature, considerate young woman who'd given someone else a chance for salvation.

"What a turn of events." Pidge winked toward her sister. "It takes a lot of guts to accept this responsibility," she said with affection and deliberation. "Especially after what these people have put you through. I'm so proud of you for coming out unscathed, and I truly think you've been given that second chance you longed for."

Seda began to fuss. A slow pink tide that changed to strawberry red bathed the new face. Pidge decided to take her downstairs.

Before going, she turned to Elena. "Dearest, one more thing."

Elena straightened.

"Please stop running back to bygone times. They're behind you, far behind you."

She nodded. "I know."

"Oh! And I almost forgot. I saw this quote the other day on Facebook and had to write it down." While holding Seda, she searched in her pocket with a free hand and found a piece of paper. "'What's done is done. And what's gone is gone,'" she read. "'One of life's most valuable lessons is learning how to let go and move on.'" She waited to gauge Elena's reaction.

"That's wonderful. It's so . . . so . . . appropriate." She raised her eyebrows in thought.

Seda had fallen asleep at Pidge's neck. "And it concluded with 'Looking back at your good memories is fine, but never let the past stop you from moving forward.'" She placed the paper back into her pocket. "You've been severely tested, darling, and you passed. In here"—she gestured at the walls with a series of nods—"this is as close as you and I are ever going to get to what we used to have." She paced toward the door, then stopped.

"It's been my mainstay," Elena said, thinning her lips.

"Listen, I want you to consider something." She paused with intention. "For me." Her face registered perseverance.

"Okay." Elena bit her bottom lip.

"Will you write yourself a letter? One that spells out all your objectives, all your worries. As best you can. You're good with words, you can do it. In it, be true to yourself."

It took a few seconds for Elena to respond to the request. "I'll think about it."

"Great."

With that, Pidge and Seda departed.

Elena Polson savored the smells, sights, and memories of the attic one last time. She would miss it dearly, but she wouldn't be able to allocate any more time or energy to using the room for quality reminiscing.

The room had served its function of containing wonderful memories. Now, however, she wouldn't have to rely on it—her tomorrows were guaranteed. The yesterdays had only been motives for the future.

From here on out, would she be less guarded, or more?

She moved again to the window and looked to the heavens. Plumes of clouds had tinged the sky white. She closed her eyes for an instant. "Mother, I'm counting on you to be my guardian angel. To look over me and Seda," she added with affection. "I'm new at this and need what help I can get."

Elena opened her eyes at the tweeting of the familiar bird that had returned to the window. She tilted her head, grinning in amazement, believing the cardinal was an omen, a sign that her mother would forever be present in some form or another.

"I love you, to eternity."

She had been rejuvenated, in a mild design of the word. A sense of security had nestled into her soul.

Her new daughter had broken the indecisions that had almost possessed her.

She reflected on how her dreams had been out of proportion. The totality of reprisals, fragilities, chaos, drama, and highs and lows had just been instrumental stepping stones to fate.

"I promise I'll remain true to my beliefs," she said. "This is my chance to no longer just exist—I'm going to live!"

Elena Polson gathered her glory and, without delay, picked up the bassinet and exited the attic. She closed the door behind her with a beam of happiness spread across her face.

Breathe in that precious air.
Hold.
Exhale the calm.
Safe.
Let go.

FROM HERE

The sound of muffled voices downstairs at her old homestead quickened Elena's footsteps. As did the aroma of coffee.

Britni waited at the landing. She was dressed in a flared lacy floral dress. She held the look of a proud surfer who had just mastered a big wave. "Hi, Grandmom!" The words were flanked by sincerity. She held a bag of new disposable diapers.

"Hey, you." Elena sat the crib down and slipped an arm around her shoulders.

There had been a subtle and immediate change in how Britni had bonded with Elena since the baby decision. To this day, the teen had no regrets about her choice; optimism had indeed turned in her direction. While other kids were trying to figure out their next step, her plan to major in drama had never wavered.

Not a surprise. May that certitude hold and bring her the assurance she longed for.

Since Seda's birth, Britni had taken a part-time job at the local civic theater, sometimes performing if a part fit her, selling tickets or helping backstage if it didn't. During her pregnancy, most of the kids at school had rallied around her, praising her bravery.

Of course, there had been bullies. But in this day and age, that was to be expected. She'd handled the predicament with courage, self-preservation, and faith in herself.

That's the kind of stuff Britni was made of.

Her home team of Elena, Hunt, and Jony applauded her progress in more ways than one. In six weeks, she would graduate from high school, and come fall, she would start the next phase of her life.

The latter Elena could relate to, so long ago. If she had the chance to live her life over, she'd cut out those wasted years and fast-forward to the present's state of mind.

But, for some reason, she'd had to endure what she'd gone through.

"Well, just dropping these off and checking in to see how things are going," Britni said, placing the diapers inside the bassinet.

Pidge appeared with the baby.

Seda's wide eyes and toothless smile enveloped the women with buoyancy as she squealed with delight.

"Hi, sugar!" Britni took Seda's tiny hand with her own, and for a brief moment, time stopped for Elena. This was one of those instances when her stomach did a flip-flop with anxiety. Her own palms developed a sweat.

However, the concern that Britni was having second thoughts was short-lived because she plunged into an animated discussion about how well her mother was doing. Jony was now a big participant in both of her children's lives, seeing Decker as much as time allowed. And to continue working in the very facility she had received treatment in took guts. Britni said her mom was studying for certification in the rehab program.

Pride was covering a lot of territory these days, ironically representing a prism. Every deviating light was fusing together.

Eighteen months ago, who would have thought any of it was possible?

Britni proceeded to the front door at the same time Pidge and Seda disappeared into the kitchen.

As Mother Nature used the western sky as a tapestry, Elena and Britni bid each other goodbye at the stoop.

"You don't know how much this means to me," Britni said before departing. Her hair had purple highlights today. "What would I have done if you and Granddad hadn't decided to take Seda?" She pursed her lips and folded her hands in front of her.

Elena savored the words. "Oh, sweetie, don't ever wonder that again, okay?" They had made a breakthrough in their improbable relationship. "We did, and that's what matters." From behind the house, the neighbor's cocker spaniel barked. "Believe me, I *do* understand how much this means.

Because . . . because you've given *me* an everlasting meaning to my life."
Tears welled up in Elena's eyes. "How can I ever thank you enough?"

The cardinal perched in a nearby bush as if to overhear the dialogue.

Britni stepped closer. "Elena, I want to apologize for all the heartache
I've caused you. I was terrible and mean." She tucked in her chin and toed
the ground. "You *were* aware that Decker and I were testing you, weren't
you?" She looked up and creased her brow.

The confession was like a clemency, a relief. In the days ahead, they
could move forward and share in the companionship of a family unit.

"Oh yes, I realize that," she replied with a snicker. "Did I pass?" She
wrung her hands.

"With flying colors!" In a surprise move, the glowing teen pecked her on
the cheek, turned, and walked away. When she had almost reached the end
of the path, she divulged over her shoulder, "I love you."

At that moment, Elena stood frozen, watching her savior carry on with
her spirited pursuits.

Who would have thought this type of scene could ever take place?

Before returning inside to her daughter and her sister, Elena felt her heart
beating in peace. Misty-eyed, she hugged herself with total bliss. None of
the challenges had been in vain. Life had only been a journey to self-
discovery.

Most notably, the emotional wounds had healed.

Heading back into Pidge's house, she promised herself to only look
ahead to each special upcoming time. Her wedding was in a few days!

Hunt was the man for her, so why resist any longer? She trusted him in
heart and soul. Her newfound family was worth every former chance,
hardship, and false start.

Hope pulsed through her.

She'd do herself a favor and wouldn't be so dependent on memories,
would give up that burden of trying to compare right now to the past. Every
so often, she had found it impossible not to associate the two.

Hadn't she waited long enough for the present?

Her sister and her partner had been right. "Don't let the bygones control
you," they had advised. "Leave it behind. Let the shadows drift away."

Yet she added her own guidance: *Treasure it true, absorb it, crowd the
past from your mind. There is no more room for regrets.*

Carry on!
She would maintain her meditation sessions but knew that aside from them, she'd no longer have to forcefully breathe in and out to get by.

She heard Pidge singing to Seda, a tune Doretta had sung to her own girls. Elena smiled with a radiance reserved only for new mothers.

Life was exactly as it should be.

***

Three days later, as a flood of sunshine engulfed Holloway Park in Worden, Ohio, Elena and Hunt were married in a decorated gazebo. The chaplain was a local pastor and former classmate of Hunt's. Only Jony, Britni, Decker, Seda, and Pidge and Bill were present. The service was basic and brief.

That evening, Elena took Pidge's advice and wrote a letter to herself. While Hunt watched television in the living room, nestled in his recliner with the baby, who was fast asleep, Elena perched her arms on the desk in her study and began to write in longhand on a lined tablet:

Dear Elena,

Well, my dear, you made it. Welcome to the twenty-first century and your rite of passage.

You've hit liberation. With a flavoring of second chances.

You've followed a path through five decades of happiness, responsibilities, adversity, freedom, laughter, mistakes, tradeoffs, discouragements, and forgiveness. It has been a designed life of endless choices. Sometimes empty, sometimes full.

As of this moment, there will be no glancing back, no wishing for "what was." You can't let the past get in your way.

You must let go. You've been disconnected much too long.

Today, you can only look to the future and enjoy the moment. You're at the right place at the right time. Redemption is so sweet!

With your new child and wonderful husband, there will be no more solitude, no more hoping for unconditional love, no heading in an aimless direction. Ironically, the Klyces saved you. Your collective support team and you are about to embark on a fresh lifetime of memories. There will be no driving in the solo lane again.

It's the beginning and you cannot wait!

This will be the only time around. No more chances will be wasted. Destiny allows only so many prospects.

Granted, you still have a lot to learn, and you're anxiously awaiting the lessons. There will be plenty to go around. As you set out on your biggest test yet, the passage is guaranteed to take a different route. As you formulate a master plan, this stretch will bring more satisfaction, more wisdom, and more perspective. A little bit of persistence and a smidge of tenacity. This is exactly where you need to be.

You CAN do this and go the distance!

Now . . . get busy!

With love,
Elena Polson Klyce

***

The next time she was at the Mortons, Elena would clip the letter to the mink wrap with care and hope one day in the future, someone would find it a treasure.

She could only pray that someone would be Seda.

Laverty Sparks

RESOURCES FOR GRANDPARENTS AS CAREGIVERS OF GRANDCHILDREN

Generations United: a Washington-based advocacy group

The National Family Caregiver Support Program: state grant program

Temporary Assistance For Needy Families: state grant program

grandfamilies.org: website that lists help available in each state

END

Laverty Sparks

ABOUT THE AUTHOR

A former advertising copywriter, Laverty is child-free, petless, but has a great support network of family and friends. She pens from her "That's All She Wrote" writing studio in the Midwest focusing on those women who know what love is all about, what works and what doesn't. Her own loves include her husband, her extended family, traveling, photography, decorating, exercising, and of course, reading.

She is also the author of contemporary romances LEATHER HORIZONS and PRIVATE PURSUITS.

You may visit her at www.laurelsparkswriting.com

Please consider leaving a review on Amazon to support the author. Thank you.

www.ingramcontent.com/pod-product-compliance
Lightning Source LLC
Chambersburg PA
CBHW020245150626
46552CB00020B/336